TH DISAPPEARED

MW01128541

Barbara Cartland

Barbara Cartland Ebooks Ltd

This edition © 2013

Book design by M-Y Books
m-ybooks.co.uk

The Barbara Cartland
Eternal Collection

The Barbara Cartland Eternal Collection is the unique opportunity to collect all five hundred of the timeless beautiful romantic novels written by the world's most celebrated and enduring romantic author.

Named the Eternal Collection because Barbara's inspiring stories of pure love, just the same as love itself, the books will be published on the internet at the rate of four titles per month until all five hundred are available.

The Eternal Collection, classic pure romance available worldwide for all time .

THE LATE DAME BARBARA CARTLAND

Barbara Cartland, who sadly died in May 2000 at the grand age of ninety eight, remains one of the world's most famous romantic novelists. With worldwide sales of over one billion, her outstanding 723 books have been translated into thirty six different languages, to be enjoyed by readers of romance globally.

Writing her first book 'Jigsaw' at the age of 21, Barbara became an immediate bestseller. Building upon this initial success, she wrote continuously throughout her life, producing bestsellers for an astonishing 76 years. In addition to Barbara Cartland's legion of fans in the UK and across Europe, her books have always been immensely popular in the USA. In 1976 she achieved the unprecedented feat of having books at numbers 1 & 2 in the prestigious B. Dalton Bookseller bestsellers list.

Although she is often referred to as the 'Queen of Romance', Barbara Cartland also wrote several historical biographies, six autobiographies and numerous theatrical plays as well as books on life, love, health and cookery. Becoming one of Britain's most popular media personalities and dressed in her trademark pink, Barbara spoke on radio and television about social and political issues, as well as making many public appearances.

In 1991 she became a Dame of the Order of the British Empire for her contribution to literature and her work for humanitarian and charitable causes.

Known for her glamour, style, and vitality Barbara Cartland became a legend in her own lifetime. Best remembered for her wonderful romantic novels and loved by millions of readers worldwide, her books remain treasured for their heroic heroes, plucky heroines and traditional values. But above all, it was Barbara Cartland's overriding belief in the positive power of love to help, heal and improve the quality of life for everyone that made her truly unique.

AUTHOR'S NOTE

The question which is so often asked about the tartan is, who is entitled to wear it? Strictly speaking the answer is that only those whose families possess tartans of their own Clan historically have a right to assume them. But, as this rule is broken by a vast majority, there is no likelihood of it being generally accepted.

In 1746 an Act was passed by the English making it illegal for Highlanders either to own or to carry arms. A year later the Dress Act was passed, making it an offence for any man or boy 'to wear or put on the clothes conveniently called Highland clothes, that is to say the plaid, philabeg or little kilt, trowse, shoulder belt or any part whatsoever of what peculiarly belongs to the Highland garb'.

For thirty-five years the hated Act remained on the statute book and the tartan was worn legally only by the Army. It was repealed in 1783, but it was first George IV and then Queen Victoria who found Scotland and Scottish dress so fascinating.

Once settled in Aberdeenshire, the Queen gave full rein to her interest in everything that concerned Highland life and Balmoral Castle was a riot of tartan.

The herbs mentioned in this story are those prescribed by the greatest herbalist of all time, Nickolas Culpepper.

Chapter One
1870

Fiona chopped up the herbs on the table in front of her until they were very small and then put them in a pan of water and set it on the old range which had been cleaned and polished until it looked comparatively new.

Everything in the kitchen seemed to shine, in spite of the fact that the room was old-fashioned with heavy beams across the ceiling.

These were hung with a large bunch of onions, a ham and in the corner a duck that had been shot yesterday by one of the neighbouring farmers.

"I've brought you this, Miss Windham," he had said to Fiona in a somewhat embarrassed manner, "as I thinks it'd make a nice meal for the little 'un."

"Thank you very much, Mr. Jarvis," Fiona had replied, knowing that his consideration was not for Mary-Rose but for herself.

She was well aware that she was greatly admired by the younger farmers in the neighbourhood, although they treated her with far too much respect to say so.

As silent tribute they brought her rabbits, pigeons, pieces of lamb and sometimes, in season, a pheasant or a brace of partridges.

Betsy usually accorded them scant ceremony when they came to the back door and, when Fiona remonstrated with her, saying how kind it was of them to trouble, she would snort derisively.

"We'd starve to death, Mary-Rose and me, if it wasn't for your pretty face!" she would say and Fiona laughingly had to acknowledge that that was the truth.

Betsy had gone down to the village shop to make some small purchases they required and Fiona, eying the brightly coloured feathers of the duck, thought that when Betsy cooked it in her own inimitable fashion, they would enjoy every mouthful.

She was wondering which of her varied recipes Betsy would choose on this occasion, when there came a loud knock on the front door.

It was so loud that Fiona suspected that whoever was outside had been pulling the bell for some time.

As this had been broken for several months, as was well known to everybody in the neighbourhood, she guessed that the caller, whoever it might be, was a stranger.

'Bother!' she said to herself.

She moved the pan to the side of the range, knowing that the one thing she must not do with herbs was to let the water boil.

That would take the goodness out of them, as she had told Betsy often enough, although the old woman would not listen to her and did everything her own way.

'Always when I am busy somebody calls,' Fiona thought testily.

Taking off the apron with which she had covered her pretty gown, she walked along the passage to the front of the house, tidying her hair as she went.

The house was very old, dating back to Elizabethan times and her sister and brother-in-law had removed a great deal of the hideous decorations and additions that had been carried out over the centuries.

Now the walls were white as they must have been when the house was first built and the paint had been scraped off the ancient ships' timbers, which the house had been built with.

The carved oak staircase now looked as it had when it was finished by the hand of some fine craftsman.

The beauty of it always pleased Fiona every time she stepped into the hall and she was appreciating it in some part of her mind even as she pulled open the front door.

Standing outside was a middle-aged man, neatly if not very fashionably dressed and behind him was a carriage drawn by two horses.

Is this the house of the late Lord Ian Rannock?" he enquired.

Fiona inclined her head.

"It is!"

"Then I wish to speak to whoever is looking after his daughter."

"I am Miss Fiona Windham and Mary-Rose is my niece."

She thought the man she was speaking to looked surprised, but he answered with only a very brief pause,

"I am delighted to meet you, Miss Windham. May I speak to you in private? My name is Angus McKeith."

Fiona opened the door a little wider.

"Please come in, Mr. McKeith."

As she spoke, she realised that his accent was Scottish.

However, it was faint and she knew that he was an educated man and undoubtedly a gentleman.

She closed the front door and, as he put his hat and travelling cape down on a chair, she walked across the hall and opened the door of the drawing room.

It was a very attractive room, low-ceilinged, with diamond-paned windows looking out onto the rose garden which lay at the back of the house. Beyond was the herb garden, which Fiona tended as her sister Rosemary had done before she died.

There were a comfortable sofa, low armchairs and flowers on almost every table which scented the room with a fragrance that mingled with the smell of the beeswax with which the floor and the ancient oak furniture were polished.

"Do sit down, Mr. McKeith," Fiona invited, indicating a chair beside the mantelpiece and seating herself in one that stood opposite.

She then sat waiting, wondering as she did so what this Scotsman had to impart and already feeling a little apprehensive of what he might say.

"May I first, Miss Windham, express my deep sympathy on the death of Lord Ian and – of course – your sister."

Mr. McKeith spoke the last two words with a slight hesitation and in a way that instinctively made Fiona stiffen.

Now she was sure that she knew why he was here and who he came from.

Because she knew that his statement required an answer, she said quietly,

"Thank you for your sympathy. It was a terrible shock."

"I can understand that," Mr. McKeith said. "It happened, I know, over a year ago, but you will appreciate that news takes some time to reach Scotland and there have been many adjustments to be made owing to Lord Ian's death."

"What adjustments?" Fiona asked bluntly.

Mr. McKeith hesitated for a moment and obviously considered his words before he replied,

"I expect, Miss Windham, that you are aware that under Scottish Law, unlike the English, a woman can inherit both the title and the estates of the Head of the Family."

If he had intended to startle Fiona he certainly succeeded.

Her blue eyes were very large in her face as she exclaimed,

"That cannot be true!"

"I can assure you it is," Mr. McKeith replied.

"Then it means – " Fiona faltered.

"That Mary-Rose is now heir-presumptive to her uncle, the Duke of Strathrannock!"

Fiona gave a little gasp as if words failed her and after a moment Mr. McKeith continued,

"You will, of course, appreciate that this means an alteration in everything that has concerned the child until now."

"Why?"

Again the question was abrupt.

"That must be obvious, Miss Windham," Mr. McKeith replied. "As long as Lord Ian was alive, the fact that he had a daughter was not of particular interest since, as he was a young man, there was every likelihood of his having a son and perhaps more than one."

"The fact that Lord Ian was heir-presumptive to his brother," Fiona remarked, "made little difference during his lifetime, since after his marriage to my sister he was completely ostracised by his family."

"It was, of course, a very unfortunate state of affairs."

Mr. McKeith spoke drily, but she sensed that he meant to be sympathetic.

"Extremely unfortunate," she replied, "and not only was my brother-in-law deeply hurt by the behaviour first of his father and then of his brother, but the insult to my sister was unforgiveable."

"I can understand only too well what you felt, Miss Windham," Mr. McKeith said, "but what happened is in the past and we now have to think of your niece, Mary-Rose."

"In what way?"

"The Duke wishes her to come to Scotland immediately."

"That is impossible."

"Why?" Mr. McKeith asked.

"Because Mary-Rose has always lived here. This is her home, where she was extremely happy with her parents. As the late Duke cut off all communication with his son and Lord Ian's brother continued in the same way, his wishes are of no particular interest to Mary-Rose or to me."

"You have constituted yourself her Guardian?" Mr. McKeith enquired.

"There was no one else to look after her when both her parents were killed," Fiona answered.

"That I understand, but I think you will find that, as Mary-Rose is now the Duke's heir-presumptive, he is legally her Guardian."

"Considering that Mary-Rose is now eight years old," Fiona retorted, "and the Duke has never made the slightest effort to see her nor shown any interest in her, I very much doubt if any English Judge would give him the Guardianship of her."

"*English* Judge?" Mr. McKeith queried. "As you are aware, Miss Windham, Mary-Rose is a Scot. The case, if it

~7~

should unfortunately come to Court, would be heard in Edinburgh."

Fiona's lips tightened and she asked with a cry in her voice,

"How can the Duke want to take Mary-Rose to Scotland? And why does he want her there? Why does he not have a child of his own? He is a young man."

There was silence and Fiona knew that Mr. McKeith was debating whether he should tell her something, but was not certain if it was the right thing for him to do.

She waited, her eyes dark and stormy, staring at the man opposite her.

"Your brother-in-law must have informed you, Miss Windham," Mr. McKeith said after a moment, "that the Duke is married."

"But I thought the Duchess was dead."

"Her Grace disappeared eight years ago, only three years after her marriage and her body has never been found. Until it is, the Duke is legally a married man."

"Can that really be so?" Fiona questioned. "I remember Ian telling me that his brother was married to a woman chosen for him by his father and that he was extremely unhappy. But I thought he was free now."

"It is a very unfortunate situation, as you can appreciate, but His Grace accepts that it is impossible for him to marry again and therefore at the moment Mary-Rose is not only his heir but the future Chieftain of the Clan."

Fiona clenched her hands together in an effort to control her voice as she said,

"Do you realise that if the Duke had made this clear when his brother was alive, it would have brought him the only thing that was missing to make his happiness complete?"

Mr. McKeith did not speak and she went on,

"My brother-in-law was deeply hurt – indeed the right word should be 'wounded' – by the fact that his brother, when he inherited, made no attempt to get in touch with him and indeed carried on the feud that had existed between Lord Ian and his father."

"The Scots are very strait-laced; Miss Windham," Mr. McKeith said, "and you must know that to them, Lord Ian's secret impetuous marriage when he was so young was a crime not only against his immediate family but against the whole Clan."

"That is nonsense!" Fiona exclaimed. "The Duke is only a few years older than Lord Ian and it was to be expected that he would produce an heir. Afterwards, when it was announced in the newspapers that the Duchess was lost and supposed dead, it was obvious that he would marry again."

She paused and added,

"I remember my brother-in-law saying, I do hope Aiden will now find someone with whom he will be as happy as I am."

"Lord Ian must have misunderstood the situation. It may seem obvious that the Duchess is dead, but, although there have been extensive searches and every possible clue to her whereabouts has been investigated, she still has to be proved dead and that appears to be an impossibility"

"It seems quite absurd to me," Fiona remarked sharply.

"It is nevertheless a fact in law," Mr. McKeith insisted.

"So now, after all these years of indifference, the Duke wishes Mary-Rose to leave her home and everything that is familiar to journey to Scotland?" Fiona asked.

"She will have a very warm welcome, Miss Windham, and I should perhaps tell you that it is the members of the Clan themselves who have asked to see her, and who wish her to be brought up in Scotland, understanding the history and traditions of the Rannocks."

"And doubtless to be indoctrinated with their feuds and cruelties to one another," Fiona said. "How can anyone trust a family who could cut one of their members out of their lives simply because he married a woman they did not approve of?"

"That question can only be answered by His Grace," Mr. McKeith replied quietly.

"Then perhaps he should come here so that I can ask him personally what he has to say about it," Fiona answered.

She saw Mr. McKeith's eyes look at her questioningly and she explained,

"I have no intention of allowing Mary-Rose to go to Scotland and certainly not alone, if that is what you intend."

Her voice was hot with anger and Mr. McKeith replied quietly,

"My instructions, Miss Windham, are to convey Mary-Rose and her nurse or Governess to Rannock Castle."

"She has neither!" Fiona snapped.

"Then the obvious person to accompany her there must be *you*, Miss Windham!"

Mr. McKeith's statement was so startling that Fiona stiffened and was very still.

Then, as she stared at him, her eyes dark with anger and very wide in her oval-shaped face, he smiled in a manner that seemed for the moment to illuminate his expression.

"I shall be interested, Miss Windham," he said, "to see if, when the time comes, you will put your case concerning Mary-Rose as bravely to His Grace as you have just put it to me."

His words seemed to release some of the tension that had held Fiona captive.

"I shall not be afraid of the Duke, if that is what you are insinuating, Mr. McKeith," she replied, "and let me make it clear, I am concerned only with the happiness of my niece, a condition which I beg leave to doubt she will find at Rannock Castle."

"That of course remains to be seen, but I would be greatly obliged, Miss Windham, if we could start our journey to Scotland as quickly as possible."

Fiona rose to her feet and walked across the room to stand at the window and look out into the garden.

She felt as if her mind was in a turmoil.

She had never expected for one moment that such a thing might happen. Because she had hated the Duke and all the Rannocks who had treated her brother-in-law so badly, she had found it wiser to make Scotland a barred subject.

Yet sometimes she had known that Ian yearned irrepressibly for the land of his birth.

When August in England was hot and airless and the garden was wilting for want of moisture, she had known by the expression in his eyes that he was thinking of the mists on the hills, of the grouse winging their way over the heather and of the burns tumbling down the glens in a silver cascade.

It was then that she would notice that her sister would be more gentle and if possible more loving than at other times, trying, Fiona was aware, to make up to her husband for all that he had given up for her.

It seemed impossible that the feud, as Fiona called it, should have continued for eight years from the moment Ian had said that he was going to marry Rosemary until he and his wife had been killed in a train accident.

At the time it had seemed an adventure to travel to London by train instead of, as they had done for years, by carriage, Ian driving with an expertise that had made Fiona long for him to have better and more expensive horseflesh.

He had in fact seemed completely content with what he possessed and never showed in any way that he regretted giving up his connection with the great castle and the huge estate known as Rannock Land for a small English manor house standing in a few acres.

It was true, Fiona had often told herself, that no two people had ever been as happy as Ian Rannock and Fiona's sister.

He had fallen in love – and she had heard the story so often – when he had least expected it and in the most unlikely circumstances.

"I was walking down Bond Street when it began to rain," he had related to Fiona. "I looked for a Hackney carriage, but, of course, there was not one to be seen. The rain looked like it was becoming a torrent, so I sought shelter in a doorway, wondering how long I would be marooned there."

He always paused at this point as if to make it more dramatic.

It was then that I heard the strains of music and realised that somebody was playing a piano. It was so beautiful and at the same time seemed so insistent that I started to listen. Then I saw that I was standing in the doorway of a Concert Hall. The rain was still teeming down so I decided I could well pass the time by listening to the music."

"And overcoming your Scottish caution about spending money, you actually bought yourself a ticket!"

"It was a small price to pay to see someone who could play so exquisitely," Ian replied.

"But you did not expect me to be a woman," Rosemary interposed at this point.

"Of course I did not!" her husband answered. "I was convinced that I would see a long-haired man and doubtless a foreigner."

"And instead?" Rosemary asked.

"I saw an angel!" he replied. "The most beautiful and exquisite angel I could ever have imagined!"

Within a week of their meeting, Fiona had been told by her sister, they were so wildly, crazily in love that there was no question of their ever again living separately.

Ian wrote to his father, announcing that he intended to marry Rosemary Windham.

Because he was in all things honest, he explained that, because she had an extraordinary musical talent and her family was hard-up, she had been persuaded to give a number of public recitals and the music critics had proclaimed her talent as exceptional, even at times using the word 'genius'.

As if Ian knew what the Duke's reaction would be, he had planned the marriage ceremony before he had received a reply.

In fact the old Duke categorically and violently forbade him to marry a woman who was "a Sassenach, an actress and doubtless at the same time a prostitute".

Ian had been shaken by the letter, even though knowing his father he had half-expected it, but Rosemary had been devastated and had clung to her father, weeping bitterly.

"How can I marry him? How can I spoil his life?" she cried. "Equally, how can I live without him?"

That had been impossible for either of them to contemplate and they had been married, Ian knowing that his father would never forgive him.

When the Duke died two years later, Ian was sure that his brother, whom he had always loved, would get in touch with him and the barrier that had prevented him from visiting his home would be lifted.

But there was no communication of any sort from the new Duke.

Gradually, Fiona knew, the hope that had risen in Ian's heart died and he faced the fact that he was exiled for life from The Castle and from his Clan, who were still, whether he wished it or not, an intrinsic part of his life.

"If only his brother could be a little more understanding," Rosemary would sometimes say to Fiona. "How could anybody cut Ian out of their life when he is so wonderful in every way?"

She gave a little sob as she added,

"He never says anything against the Duke. He is never bitter and yet I know in my heart how much he minds."

Thinking of this now, Fiona told herself that the Duke of Strathrannock must be an insensitive brutal man.

Being a Scot, he must understand just how much Scotland meant to his brother and yet he could go on punishing him for loving a woman who was in fact not an actress but rather a very gifted musician.

Because she hoped that it would make relations better between Ian and his father, Rosemary had given up her public career as soon as they were married.

She played now only to her husband and her sister and later, as she grew older, to her daughter.

It was a deep sadness to both Ian and Rosemary that they had only one child, but Mary-Rose was so angelic in every way, a 'dream-child', her father called her, that she completely made up for the lack of brothers and sisters.

Now, when Fiona was thinking of her, almost as if she had drawn her by her thoughts, the door of the drawing room opened and Mary-Rose came into the room.

"Aunt Fiona!" she cried in her lilting voice. "I have found the honeysuckle you wanted. See, I have a whole basket of it!"

She ran across the room without being aware that anyone was sitting by the fireside and Fiona turned from the window.

As she had done so often, she thought that her niece looked like a small angel who had just dropped out of Heaven.

Ian Rannock had thought that Rosemary looked like an angel when he had first seen her sitting at the piano on the stage of the Concert Hall, seeming too small to evoke so much sound from a grand piano – and Mary-Rose was the creation of their love.

Delicately boned, with a small round face and large blue eyes set wide apart, she had hair rioting about her head in curls that were the colour of the first fingers of dawn.

It was impossible for anybody who saw Mary-Rose for the first time not to stop and look at her and then look again and Fiona could see now the astonishment in Mr. McKeith's eyes.

"That was very clever of you, darling!" she said as she took the basket of honeysuckle from Mary-Rose. "And now I want you to say how-do-you-do to a gentleman who has come all the way from Scotland to meet you."

Mary-Rose gave a little start – then, seeing Mr. McKeith, she walked across the room to him.

She dropped him a little curtsey and held out her hand.

"I'm sorry I didn't notice you when I came into the room," she said, "but I was so excited at finding the honeysuckle that Aunt Fiona wanted for her magic herbs."

Mr. McKeith rose a little laboriously to his feet to stand holding Mary-Rose's hand in his.

"Magic herbs?" he questioned. "What are they?"

"Herbs that make people well when they are ill! Some people think Aunt Fiona is a 'White Witch'!"

Mary-Rose laughed as she spoke and it made her look even more like a small angel than she did already.

Fiona drew in her breath.

"Mr. McKeith, dearest, wishes us to travel to Scotland with him so that you can meet your uncle, the Duke of Strathrannock."

"Would that be Dadda's brother?" Mary-Rose asked.

"Yes," Mr. McKeith answered.

"I know all about Uncle Aiden," Mary-Rose went on. "He lives in a big castle where Dadda used to play as a little boy. It has towers where the Rannocks fought to keep away the wicked invaders who wanted to steal their cattle and sheep."

Fiona was astonished.

"Did your Mama tell you that?" she asked.

"No, it was Dadda," Mary-Rose replied. "When we were alone, he would tell me stories of Scotland and his home and what he did when he was the same age as me."

Fiona understood then that Ian had felt he must talk to someone about the land he loved, the place where he had been born and bred.

To do so to his wife would make her unhappy because Rosemary would then feel how much he had given up for her. So he had talked to Mary-Rose, although until this moment Fiona had no idea of it.

"I am sure you will find it very interesting, Mary-Rose," Mr. McKeith said, "to see The Castle where your father was born and to meet the people who loved him when he was a boy."

"Are we really going to Scotland?" Mary-Rose asked.

"You would like that?"

"It would be very exciting! But I couldn't go without Aunt Fiona "

"She will travel with you and stay with you at The Castle."

Fiona was feeling that, although he spoke reassuringly, there was a momentary mental reserve behind the words that he did not say aloud.

'I will not let the Duke take Mary-Rose away from me,' she thought fiercely.

She told herself that she had always hated him and now her feeling for him was one of positive loathing.

"Does Uncle Aiden look like Dadda?" Mary-Rose enquired.

"I think you will see a resemblance," Mr. McKeith answered. "But His Grace is a few years older than your father and he has not been happy in his life."

"Why not?" Mary-Rose asked.

"I think the answer is that he does not possess a daughter like you," Mr. McKeith said with a smile.

"That means he is lonely," Mary-Rose reflected wisely. "Mama said we must always be very kind to people who are lonely, like poor old Mr. Benson in the village, whose wife died and whose son was killed in a battle."

"Then I hope you will be kind to your uncle," Mr. McKeith said.

"I'll try," Mary-Rose promised. "It'll be very exciting to see the big walls and the towers that Dadda told me about. They are still – there?"

She asked the question anxiously and Mr. McKeith assured her that they were.

*

Afterwards, Fiona found it very difficult to remember her feelings, much less to analyse them, as she packed up the house that had been her home for the last five years and where she had expected to stay indefinitely looking after Mary-Rose.

She was sixteen when her father had died and she had found herself alone.

She and Rosemary had lost their mother when they were small children and their father had never been the same after her death.

He had been comparatively elderly when he had married for the second time and started a family, having had no children by his first wife.

He adored his two beautiful daughters, but his health was frail and it was really because they needed money for the expensive treatment he was having and the special food the doctors had ordered for him that Rosemary had exploited her talent at the pianoforte by playing in public.

She had given only four recitals when she met Ian, but she had made enough money after the first one, which was a huge success, to keep her father in comparative comfort until his death.

After that, it had been obvious that there was nowhere else for Fiona to live but with her sister.

She had been a little afraid that Ian would resent her making a fourth – counting Mary-Rose – in their happy household, but, because she was very tactful and never intruded when she knew that husband and wife wished to be alone, the whole arrangement worked out well.

The nanny who had looked after Mary-Rose when she was a baby had left and Fiona had constituted herself as nurse and Governess to her small niece.

"You can teach her music," she had said to her sister, "and Ian can teach her botany, for no one knows more about trees, flowers and wildlife than he does, but I will teach her everything else."

Because their father had been a scholarly man and they had both had a good education, Fiona was fully qualified to teach and Mary-Rose, being intelligent, was quick to learn.

She had also found that the child's mind was as original and entrancing as her looks.

It was, Fiona thought, as if, because her sister and her husband were so in love with each other, they had produced a child so lovely both in body and mind that Mary-Rose might indeed have been the angel she appeared to be.

Because she was happy she wanted to give happiness and because her mother had taught her that it was a gift to be given, small though she was, she was sympathetic and understanding to other people's troubles.

'How can the Duke, who has obviously never thought of anyone but himself, be the right type of Guardian for a childlike Mary-Rose?' Fiona asked herself a thousand times.

She packed up the items her sister had treasured, amongst them a number of religious books, which had always lain beside her bed and a picture of angels playing with the Child Jesus which had hung over Mary-Rose's.

She knew a little about religious practice in Scotland and was sure that it was bleak and harsh and she shivered at what lay ahead.

Mary-Rose, on the other hand, was thrilled at the thought of seeing The Castle and she plied Mr. Mc-Keith with question after question, surprising him with the intelligence of them and the humanity in everything she said and thought.

Because Betsy was quite content to stay on at The Manor as caretaker, Fiona was relieved that it was not the same as feeling that she had lost her home forever.

The Manor now belonged to Mary-Rose, but it would have been impossible for her to live there if the small amount of money Fiona had inherited on her father's death had not contributed to the upkeep of the house and all the other expenses.

Lord Ian had very little money during his lifetime and what he did own had been left him by his grand-mother.

When he married Rosemary, the Duke in traditional fashion cut him off without a penny.

In consequence it had been hard at times to make ends meet, but somehow they had managed. Fiona now found herself wondering how it would be possible for her even to be polite to the Duke when she saw the contrast between his way of life and that of her sister.

At the same time she had no intention of giving up her Guardianship of Mary-Rose.

She had a feeling that it would be hard to transplant anything so sweet and delicate from the soft gentleness of the South to the harsh climate of the North.

'If things are too bad,' she told herself, 'I will take Mary-Rose away with me whatever the Duke may say. Then let him fight out the question of Guardianship in the Courts. I am sure it will take years and perhaps Scottish Law cannot be enforced in England.'

She would have liked to consult a Solicitor before she left for Scotland, but that was impossible since Mr. McKeith, although he was very polite and did not press her, was obviously extremely anxious to return to The Castle as quickly as possible.

'He will have to wait until I am ready,' Fiona told herself firmly.

At the same time she felt him there all the time, forcing her to make haste while every instinct in her told her to linger.

Mr. McKeith was in fact a charming and extremely intelligent man.

They talked together in the evenings after Mary-Rose had gone to bed and Fiona found him interesting and understanding.

"I know it is hard for you to adjust yourself to the present situation, Miss Windham," he said, "but you must realise that from Mary-Rose's point of view, the position she will occupy as the Duke's heir is almost the equivalent in England to being the Princess Royal."

Fiona looked at him enquiringly and he went on,

"A Duke in Scotland – and the Duke of Strathrannock is one of the most important of them – is Head of his Clan and rules over his own estates and his own people almost as if he was a King."

"I have heard that," Fiona murmured.

"As you know," Mr. McKeith continued, "The Castle is on the border where it was erected hundreds of years ago as a defence against the English. It is the Scottish counterpart of Alnwick Castle in Northumberland, where the Percys defied the marauding Scots."

He smiled as he went on,

"The Duke also owns land in other parts of Scotland and his prestige and that of his Clan is well known over the whole country."

"The Duke is obviously very wealthy," Fiona remarked.

There was no need for Mr. McKeith to reply.

He knew she was thinking that many of the carpets and curtains in The Manor house were threadbare, that the two horses in the stables were inferior animals and that the carriage her sister and Ian had used was sadly out of date.

After a moment Mr. McKeith remarked,

"Second sons always suffer at any level of Society, Miss Windham. I speak with experience, for I was one myself."

"It is unfair!"

"So are a lot of things in life."

"Injustice always makes me very angry."

Mr. McKeith gave a little laugh.

"Then may I beg you, Miss Windham, not to vent your anger on me, but keep it for the Duke"

""That is exactly what I intend to do," Fiona exclaimed.

*

As if to give her a taste of what lay ahead, she learnt, on the day that she and Mary-Rose were to leave The Manor, that they would drive to the nearest railway station, which was some fifteen miles away, where the Duke's private train would be waiting to convey them to Scotland.

"Private train?" Fiona enquired.

"It is a comparatively new toy," Mr. McKeith said a little cynically. "The Duke considers it important both for his comfort and his status amongst the other Dukes."

If Fiona was astonished, Mary-Rose was entranced.

The train, painted white with the Rannock coat of arms on the engine, looked much more like a toy than a genuine train.

There were several Stewards in attendance and they were all wearing the Rannock livery until they neared the North, when they changed, to Mary-Rose's delight, into kilts of the Rannock tartan.

There were comfortable armchairs in the saloon and brass bedsteads in the sleeping compartments.

"Dadda never told me about this lovely train," Mary-Rose remarked.

"It is new," Fiona explained. "When your father was a small boy he had to travel down from the North behind horses. I remember him telling me what a long drive it was and how tired he was when he finally arrived in London."

"I would have liked to be on the train with Dadda," Mary-Rose said, "but I expect, now that he's in Heaven, he can see me in it and knows how comfortable I am."

"I am sure he can," Fiona answered. "Now say your prayers, dearest and then try to go to sleep. There will be lots of exciting scenes to watch from the windows tomorrow."

She sat down beside the bed and Mary-Rose knelt on it and put her hands together.

She said the prayers she had always said ever since her mother had taught them to her almost as soon as she could speak.

Then she added,

"Thank you, God, for sending me in this lovely train to see The Castle where Dadda played when he was a little boy and please tell Dadda to look down and see everything I'm doing in case I miss something he told me about."

She said 'amen' and cuddled down in the bed as Fiona, hiding her tears, tucked her up.

When she was with Mary-Rose, she missed her sister more than at any other time.

Although Rosemary had been much older than Fiona, they had been very close and not a day passed when Mary-Rose did not remind her of the happiness she and her sister had found in each other's company.

It was Ian who had suggested that they should turn the name round from Rosemary to Mary-Rose.

"She is a little replica of you, my darling," he had said before the Christening, "and, whatever we call her, to me she will always be another Rosemary."

"If she had been a son I would have wanted to call him Ian," Rosemary whispered, "because no man could be anything but wonderful if he has your name."

"I have an idea!" Ian exclaimed. "To call her Rosemary would be really too muddling, so she must be Mary-Rose."

His wife had clapped her hands together.

"That is perfect, and so clever of you," she said. "Oh, darling, you must just promise me one thing, not to love her more than you love me or I might be jealous."

"Do you think that is possible?" Ian asked. "I love you until you fill the world, the sky and the whole universe and, if Mary-Rose when she grows up is half as happy as we are, then I ask nothing more for her."

Fiona felt as if at the Christening Service there had been celestial beings listening as the Parson held the small babe in his arms and made the sign of the cross on her forehead.

Mary-Rose had smiled at him and seemed to enjoy every minute of it.

"There is one thing certain," someone had said when they returned to The Manor, "the Devil has not come out of her."

"And a very good thing too," Ian replied with a twinkle in his eyes. "Every woman needs a touch of the Devil in her if she is to hold her own in this world!"

Fiona, who had been only thirteen years old at the time, had not quite understood what he meant, but her father, who also was at the Christening, had chuckled and said,

"You are quite right. Women who are too good and complacent are a bore and a man needs to be stimulated now and then. I am quite certain my granddaughter will do that when the time comes."

"Nonsense," Rosemary protested firmly. "She looks like an angel and she will be one – just like me."

They had all laughed at that, but later Fiona often thought that both she and her sister had a touch of the Devil in them.

Rosemary very rarely showed it, the reason being that she was so happy with her husband, but Fiona had a temper and, as she told Mr. McKeith, where there was injustice it burst into flames inside her.

She once had discovered a boy torturing a small dog and, although he was larger than she was, she had set about him with a stick until he had run away, frightened at her violence.

She told herself now that there was a Devil in herself, which she tried to control, but when she met the Duke she would tell him a few home truths.

"He is rich, with a castle in Scotland, estates in other parts of the country and a private train, while his brother had to count every penny. It's not fair."

"It's not fair!"

"It's not fair!"

The wheels of the train seemed to pick up the words until they ran through her mind like a refrain.

"It 's not fair!"

Chapter Two

"We should arrive at Rannock Station in about twenty minutes," Mr. McKeith announced.

Fiona gave a little start and felt, although it irritated her, that her heart was beating unaccountably quickly.

She knew it was nervousness and she despised herself for being nervous of anything, especially of the Duke.

The journey had been very enjoyable and Mary-Rose had found it irresistible to be able to run along the whole length of the train with its communicating carriages.

Fiona had read that in all the new trains this was possible, but it was only the previous year, she learnt, that the Queen had abandoned the old Royal railway coach for a new small one with all the compartments communicating.

At last there would be no more steep clambering down onto the line for the Ladies-in-Waiting to reach the Queen, which had always been considered very indelicate, for it was impossible to do so without exposing a great deal of leg.

For Mary-Rose it had been an absorbing game to run from one end of the train to the other and now as she came towards Fiona she called out,

"We are going to arrive very soon, Aunt Fiona."

"That is just what I was going to tell you," Fiona replied with a smile.

"I'll be sorry to leave this lovely train," Mary-Rose sighed, "but then I do want to see The Castle."

The idea of The Castle had captured her imagination and Fiona knew that Mr. McKeith had deliberately spent a great deal of time in telling her of the history of it and the many battles that had been fought there by the Rannocks in the past.

Last night when Fiona had heard her prayers and was tucking her up in bed, Mary-Rose had asked,

"If Dadda had lived, would he have been a Duke?"

"Only if your uncle did not have any children," Fiona replied.

"Why hasn't Uncle Aiden any children?" Mary-Rose questioned.

This was difficult to answer and Fiona compromised with the truth by saying,

"Your uncle has no wife at the moment."

"If he married and had a little girl like me, I would not be his heir?"

She was obviously puzzling it out for herself and Fiona thought that it was rather tiresome of Mr. McKeith to have worried her with the problems that were waiting for them at The Castle.

At the same time she knew that he was preparing her for the position to which she was entitled and she could not help feeling that it was very bitter that her brother-in-law, who would have enjoyed every moment of it, had been left in the wilderness while Mary-Rose now took her place.

It did not improve her already antagonistic feelings towards the Duke, but she told herself that the only thing that really mattered was Mary-Rose's happiness.

She was certain that this meant that she must stay with her and not leave her alone in the charge of her Rannock relations.

'If I am too disagreeable,' she told herself, 'the Duke will send me away. I must be careful. Equally I have no intention of toadying to him or letting him think that I am not horrified at his behaviour, because I am!'

She tidied Mary-Rose's fair curls, put her bonnet over them and tied the blue ribbons, which matched her eyes, under her little chin.

The blue coat which covered her long white gown made her look as if she had stepped out of a painting and Fiona wondered with a twist of her lips whether the Duke would appreciate his niece's beauty.

She had a feeling that simple though their clothes were, she and Mary-Rose would look, to the dour Scots, like creatures from another world.

She had seen pictures in the ladies' magazines of the drab heavy tweeds that women wore in Scotland and she knew that, even if she had wanted to dress like that, she could not at the moment have afforded to.

There were quite a number of expenses before she had left The Manor and she had been obliged to draw out almost all the money she had in the bank, out of which Betsy's wages could be paid regularly.

It had also been impossible to dismiss the old gardener, who had been with her sister and brother-in-law ever since they had married. He was getting on towards seventy and it would have been impossible for him to find other employment.

She knew that he had been extremely relieved when she had told him to help Betsy take care of The Manor and that his wages would still be paid even while there was no one living in it.

This left her in what she knew was a precarious position financially and she therefore thought, with a toss of her head, that the Duke could put up with the clothes she had worn in the South and if he did not like them there was nothing she could do about it.

As Fiona and Rosemary had been about the same size, Fiona had had no compunction about adding Rosemary's wardrobe to her own.

In fact she loved to wear her sister's clothes, feeling that it somehow brought her nearer and that, when she was wearing one of Rosemary's favourite gowns, she could almost talk to her as if she was in the room.

Lord Ian had liked his wife to be very feminine and, because Rosemary was fair and blue-eyed like their daughter, he preferred her in white or in the soft blues which he told her made her look like love-in-a-mist.

Fiona was thinking of her sister now as she buttoned down the front of the little velvet coat she wore over her attractive gown, which swirled out in a bustle behind her and was finished with a large bow of satin ribbon.

Because she was suddenly conscious of her appearance, she thought that Mr. McKeith glanced at her a little apprehensively and she was sure that he was wondering what the Duke would say when he saw her.

As the train began to slow down, Fiona said in a low voice,

"Have you told His Grace that I am coming with Mary-Rose?"

He hesitated before he spoke.

Then she saw that his eyes were twinkling.

"I am not going to admit that I was too cowardly to do so," he replied, "but I have always found it wisest in life not to anticipate trouble."

"And that is what you are expecting?"

"You know His Grace is expecting Mary-Rose to be accompanied by a nurse or a Governess – "

"Then you must explain to him that I am both," Fiona pointed out quickly.

He glanced at the elegant little hat trimmed with roses that she wore on her head and she knew, without his saying so that he was thinking she did not look in the least like a nurse or a Governess.

'Whatever he may say,' she thought to herself, 'I know that he is afraid of the Duke and I expect everybody else is too.'

Her chin went up a little as she thought that the Windhams, who, whatever their faults, had never been cowardly.

"We are here! *We are here!*" Mary-Rose was crying, jumping up and down with excitement and clapping her hands.

The train drew to a halt at the small station, which Fiona learnt had been built entirely to serve The Castle.

Their private train had left the main line an hour or so earlier and had been moving through country that was wild and beautiful, which was called, Mr. McKeith had told her, the Border Country.

Looking out of the window, Fiona thought of the battles that had raged to and fro across the Scottish and English border and how many men had died as the two countries opposed each other with a hatred that even now she was sure still smouldered in many hearts.

Had not the old Duke, in his letter to his son, given as his first reason for refusing to permit the marriage that Rosemary was a Sassenach, the contemptuous term used by the Scots to describe the English?

'To the present Duke, I suppose that too is a crime,' she told herself.

She thought that, if the Scots had hated the English, the English hated them no less.

She remembered that Alnwick Castle, which guarded the English side of the border, had been surrendered to David, King of Scotland, in 1138.

It was one of the dates she always remembered, having learnt it from her father, who had been in his own way just as fanatical an English patriot as the old Duke had been a Scottish one.

It was annoying to remember that the Scottish Armies had been victorious at the Battle of the Standard and she suspected that their victory had been celebrated in Rannock Castle.

For generation after generation the Armies had fought each other and not until now was there peace between the two countries, except in the hearts of men like the Duke of Strathrannock.

The train came to a standstill and through the windows Fiona could see men, wearing kilts, waiting for them on the small platform.

They all wore the green and blue Rannock tartan with a red line running through it, and on their heads were bonnets trimmed with blackcocks' feathers.

Mary-Rose slipped her hand into Fiona's and she knew that the child was excited to the point where she could no longer speak.

Mr. McKeith rose to his feet and, as they walked to the door of the compartment, Fiona said,

"Perhaps you should go first. There seems to be a large number of people to meet us."

"They are mostly the servants," Mr. McKeith replied, "but I suspect some of the Clansmen are too curious to wait to see Mary-Rose at The Castle."

He put out his hand to the child and suggested,

"Come with me and meet some of the people who bear the same name as yourself, many of whom knew your father as a boy and loved him."

Mary-Rose, who was never shy, went with him.

He stepped down onto the platform and lifted her in his arms.

Then there was a shout of welcome from the waiting Scotsmen who crowded round to stare at Mary-Rose.

Holding the child by the hand, Mr. McKeith introduced her to a number of the more elderly servants.

"This is Donald," Fiona heard him say, "Chief Ghillie to His Grace. He will tell you how your father caught his first salmon when he was the same age as you are now."

There were ghillies, keepers, foresters, stalkers and dozens of others. Mary-Rose shook them by the hand and some of the older men stared at her with what was suspiciously like tears in their eyes.

Then they stepped into open carriages, which were waiting outside the station and were driven away over land that Fiona had to admit was very beautiful.

There were large pinewoods, silver streams winding through the moorland and, although the heather was not yet purple, it was unmistakably a Scottish landscape.

In the distance there were mountains, which were slightly indistinct owing to the mist that hung over them.

Fiona wanted to ask Mr. McKeith their names so that later she could look them up on a map, but Mary-Rose was talking so excitedly about everything that she did not wish to interrupt the child.

It was not surprising that the little girl was thrilled, for they passed through several small hamlets and the inhabitants, from the elderly to the children, were all lining the roadway to wave and cheer as their carriage appeared.

To Fiona it seemed extraordinary that Mary-Rose could cause such excitement, but, when she looked enquiringly at Mr. McKeith, he explained,

"We are on Rannock land and there will be no one who is unaware of who is arriving today. Lord Ian was very popular – I think everybody loved him."

Fiona pressed her lips together to prevent herself from making the sarcastic retort that rose to her mind.

Then a minute or so later Mary-Rose gave a cry of excitement and Fiona realised that she was pointing ahead to The Castle, which was now in sight.

She had expected it to be magnificent, but not as large and impressive as it actually was.

Now she understood why it had dominated Ian's childhood and indeed his whole life.

The first Lord Rannock had begun to build The Castle in 1030 and had been succeeded by his son and his grandson, who spent the whole of their lives in war against the English.

Perpetual warfare, Fiona had learnt, had by the year 1300 reduced the inhabitants of the Border Lands to a condition of misery, but the Scots were in the ascendant and Edward III of England led a large Army into the North to drive them back. The English went on winning until King David of Scotland was taken prisoner and they invaded Scotland, burning several towns, including

Edinburgh, and laying waste to all the country they passed through.

The Scots, led by a Rannock who desired to avenge their miseries, in their turn devastated Northumberland and the warfare on the border continued.

Fiona knew that The Castle had been a place of refuge to all who had lived in the surrounding countryside.

She had heard Mr. McKeith telling Mary-Rose that there were always scouts on duty all along the border and, whenever they saw an English Army or a foraging party approaching, they lit a succession of beacons.

These warned the Rannocks to hurry, with their families, their cattle and all other livestock into the shelter of The Castle.

As they drew nearer to it, Fiona could see the huge stone wall that encircled it and she knew how protective and comforting it must have seemed to those to whom it gave sanctuary.

At intervals along the wall, which was extremely high, stood towers that must have concealed hundreds of soldiers who could shoot from the narrow, arrow-slit windows where their enemies were unable to hurt them.

Originally The Castle had been entirely surrounded by a deep moat, but now, Mr. McKeith told Fiona, all that was left of it lay below the North wall.

"We will enter by the middle gateway," Mr McKeith proposed as they drew nearer still. "It's the nearest point of entry to the part of The Castle where the Duke lives."

"It is very very big!" Mary-Rose cried.

"As I told you, it had need to be," Mr. McKeith replied.

They passed through the gateway and could see that a large expanse of green and well-tended ground lay inside the high walls.

"When the people were sheltered in here," he went on, speaking to Mary-Rose, "they knew there were soldiers to protect them and so they would camp with their cattle on the ground which is now covered with grass."

Mary-Rose looked round her excitedly as Mr. McKeith pointed out the Clock Tower, the Falconer's Tower, the Postern Tower and the Constable's Tower.

Now they were within the walls and driving towards The Castle itself, which stood in the centre, its crenelated parapets surmounted by lead statues.

They passed through another gateway between two high towers and drew up beside a flight of steps at the top of which was a huge oak-studded door.

For their approach a red carpet had been laid down the steps and on each side of it there stood servants dressed in their kilts and wearing coats emblazoned with crested silver buttons.

An impressive Major Domo stood at the top of the steps and, as Mr. McKeith led Mary-Rose up them, he said in stentorian tones,

"Welcome back, sir, and welcome to you, Miss Mary-Rose! 'Tis glad we all be to see you!"

"Thank you very much," Mary-Rose said, holding out her hand.

He was obviously touched by the gesture and took it, bending his head low, as if in reverence.

Then, still leading Mary-Rose, Mr. McKeith started to climb up the wide stone staircase, which was hung with antlers' horns and tattered flags that had once been captured in battle.

Also on the walls, making a magnificent pattern over the chimneypiece, were the shields and claymores that had been used in the past.

There was so much to look at that Fiona wanted to stop and stare, but submissively she followed Mr. McKeith and Mary-Rose, feeling that because she was English she had been quickly relegated to her proper place.

At the top of the stairs there was a landing and opening off it were several pairs of double mahogany doors.

Fiona remembered that Ian had told her that in Scotland the important rooms were all on the first floor and she was therefore not surprised when the Major Domo, who had gone ahead of them, flung open two doors and announced in a voice that seemed to ring out almost like a clarion call,

"Miss Mary-Rose Rannock, Your Grace!"

As he spoke, Mr. McKeith relinquished Mary-Rose's hand and stood just inside the doorway, while the child edged forward towards a man at the far end of the room.

He stood in front of a chimneypiece of carved stone, which soared high towards the ceiling and seemed to make a perfect background for its present owner.

Without really meaning to do so, Fiona stopped beside Mr. McKeith and stared at the Duke.

Fiona had expected him to be impressive, she had expected that because she was so sure that Ian resembled him he would be handsome, but she had not thought that he would be quite so magnificent or so overpowering.

Dressed in a kilt with a silver-topped sporran, he seemed to be a giant of a man and she learnt later that he was in fact all of six foot three inches in height.

There was a distinct resemblance to his brother in his dark hair and straight eyebrows over grey eyes.

But the expression on his face was so different that had she seen him in different circumstances Fiona wondered if she would have guessed that he was Lord Ian's brother.

He looked imperious, authoritative, reserved or perhaps the right word was cold.

There was nothing warm or human about him and Fiona told herself that he could undoubtedly be ruthless and perhaps cruel.

He stood utterly at his ease, watching the small figure of Mary-Rose advance towards him.

Fiona felt that there was no softness in his eyes, only a cynicism and perhaps even dislike – she could not be sure.

Then the spell that seemed to have kept Mary-Rose silent yet had compelled her to walk towards the Duke broke and, with a little cry that was characteristic of her, she exclaimed,

"You *are* like Dadda! I can see it now and he told me that you looked just like each other when you were little boys."

She reached the Duke and tipped her head up to stare at him.

"This is a very big castle, Uncle Aiden, but Dadda said that, when you were little like me, you climbed up all the Towers to the very top. Will I be able to do that?"

There was something so compelling in the childish voice that it seemed as if she broke through the Duke's reserve and he bent down towards her, holding out his hand.

"Perhaps first, Mary-Rose, we should say how-do-you-do to each other and let me welcome you to my home."

"I'm sorry – I forgot to curtsey," Mary-Rose exclaimed, doing so as she spoke.

Then she put her hand in the Duke's and said,

"It's difficult for you to kiss me when I am wearing my bonnet, so perhaps you had better lift me up to do so."

In any circumstances, Fiona told herself, she would have been amused by the expression on the Duke's face. She knew it had never crossed his mind for an instant that he should kiss his niece.

A little awkwardly he bent down and picked her up in his arms.

Confidingly Mary-Rose put her arm round his neck and said,

"That's better! You're very tall!"

Then she kissed his cheek.

"I think the answer to that is that you are very small," the Duke replied, as if he had to assert himself.

"I expect I'll grow," Mary-Rose laughed, "just as you did."

"That is true," the Duke admitted.

As if feeling slightly embarrassed at holding Mary-Rose, he set her down on the floor and turned to Mr. McKeith.

"I am glad you are back, McKeith. You seem to have been away for a long time and there is a great deal of work waiting for you."

"I am sure there is, Your Grace."

Mr. McKeith walked forward after the Duke had spoken to him and Fiona accompanied him.

Only when they reached the hearthrug where the Duke was standing did he appear to notice Fiona for the first time and there was no mistaking the surprise in his eyes.

"Who is this?" he enquired.

"May I present Miss Fiona Windham, Your Grace."

"Windham?"

The question was sharp.

"I am Mary-Rose's aunt," Fiona said briefly as she curtseyed.

The Duke raised his eyebrows.

"You thought it necessary to bring your niece here to The Castle?"

"There was no one else," Fiona replied. "Mr. McKeith told me that you wished her to be accompanied by her nurse or her Governess and, as it happens, I am both, besides having a nearer relationship."

She thought that there was an expression of anger in the Duke's eyes as he said,

"Did my brother employ you in that capacity?"

Fiona felt that he intended to be rude and her eyes were steely as she replied quietly,

"Your brother and my sister, Your Grace, lived in very straitened circumstances and had no money to employ a large staff. When I went to live with them after my father's death, I was only too pleased to make myself useful by looking after and teaching Mary-Rose."

It seemed as if the Duke found this hard to believe, but he asked in a voice that Fiona was certain would have intimidated most people,

"Are you expecting to stay here?"

"I feel certain that is what Mary-Rose would wish me to do," Fiona replied.

The child, who had not been listening to the exchange that was taking place, was suddenly aware of what was being said and she turned to the Duke to say,

"Please, Uncle Aiden, I want Aunt Fiona to stay with me. I'd be very unhappy if she went away and she teaches me many things I want to know."

There was no mistaking the plea in the childish voice and, as if the Duke found it difficult to make a decision without further consideration, he said a little cynically,

"I am sure that for the moment at any rate we can accommodate your aunt in The Castle."

"Would you like me to take Mary-Rose and Miss Windham to their rooms, Your Grace?" Mr. McKeith asked.

"I think that would be a good idea and, of course, I hope to see my niece later in the evening."

The way he excluded her was pointed, Fiona thought, but she merely curtseyed gracefully and turned to follow Mr. McKeith, holding out her hand to Mary-Rose as she did so.

But Mary-Rose had something else to say,

"Uncle Aiden, will you show me the places that you and Dadda used to hide in when you were naughty, so that no one could find you? I want to go to the Guard Tower where once you – defied your Tutor and refused to do any lessons."

She gave a little gurgle of laughter.

"That must have been fun! Dadda said he was very very angry when you stayed right at the top of the Tower and he was too old to clamber up the steps and catch you."

"Now listen to me, Mary-Rose," the Duke said, "and this is important!"

There was a note of authority in his voice that swept the smile from Mary-Rose's lips.

"You are never," the Duke continued, "never in any circumstances – do you understand – to go to the Guard Tower. You can play anywhere else in The Castle and in the grounds, but the Guard Tower is not safe. I intend to have it repaired, but it has not yet been done and so you are to keep away from it. Do you understand?"

Mary-Rose gave a little sigh.

"Yes, Uncle Aiden, I understand, but perhaps I can look up and see where you sat on top of the Tower without going inside it."

"Yes, you can do that," the Duke said. "But remember what I have just told you and it would be wise for your – aunt to remember it too."

There was a little pause before the word 'aunt', as if he found it difficult to admit the relationship and Fiona continued,

"I shall not forget, Your Grace, but you will understand that because Mary-Rose's father loved his home very deeply, he told her stories about it which she will always remember."

Fiona thought her words would make the Duke feel embarrassed, but he only looked at her in what she thought was a somewhat contemptuous manner.

Then Mary-Rose ran to her and put her hand in hers.

"It's all very exciting, isn't it, Aunt Fiona?" she asked as they walked down the room. "And Uncle Aiden does look a little like Dadda, but older and rather – fierce!"

They had reached the door by this time, but Fiona was quite certain that the Duke had heard the child's description of him.

She hoped it made him feel uncomfortable, although she doubted it.

They were introduced by Mr. McKeith to an elderly housekeeper and taken to rooms on the same floor, but which were a long way down a twisting passage and were, Fiona decided, in one of the other Towers,

There was a large room for Mary-Rose with a four-poster bed that delighted her and a room opening out of it for Fiona. It had been intended, she knew, for Fiona's Governess. It was therefore not as impressive as the one the child would occupy.

However, it was quite comfortable and had a magnificent view from the window over the encircling wall of The Castle and the wild moorland beyond it.

"I'll send one of the housemaids to unpack for you, miss," Mrs. Meredith, the housekeeper said. "Her name is Jeannie and she'll look after you and the wee bairn."

Her voice softened as she looked at Mary-Rose, who was exploring her room.

Then she added,

"It be happy day for us all to see his Lordship's daughter and know she's to live amongst us."

"I think Lord Ian would like to know she is here," Fiona said softly.

"We've missed him! We've missed him awful all these years," Mrs. Meredith said, "and many a tear was shed over the whole countryside when it was learnt he'd met his death in one of those mechanical monsters they call trains!"

"It was very sad for Mary-Rose to lose her father and mother both at the same time," Fiona replied.

"We'll make it up to her. She's come home, and there's no one who calls himself a Rannock who'll not be ready to fight and die for her!"

Fiona wanted to say that she hoped they would have to do nothing of the sort, but she knew that the old woman was speaking with a deep sincerity and she could only smile her thanks.

The luggage was brought upstairs and Jeannie came to unpack for them, exclaiming with delight at Fiona's gowns as she hung them up in the ancient carved oak wardrobe.

Mary-Rose, however, soon became restless.

"Please, Aunt Fiona, I want to see more of The Castle," she pleaded. "Let's go and find Uncle Aiden and tell him what we want to do."

"I don't think we should disturb your uncle, dearest. It will soon be your bedtime, but as it is such a lovely evening, I think we might have a little walk outside before your supper is ready."

Fiona instructed Jeannie to prepare a bath and told her what Mary-Rose should have for supper.

Then, because it seemed foolish to dress up just to go out for a few minutes, they went down the stairs as they were and out onto the green grass that looked like a velvet carpet surrounding the main castle.

Mary-Rose, however, was intent on seeing the Guard Tower which she had heard so much about from her father.

Fiona knew that it had captured her imagination because the two young boys – she supposed they must have been about ten and thirteen at the time – had been so naughty as to defy authority.

It was the sort of story that any child would find fascinating and Mary-Rose could repeat word by word what she had been told.

"They took food from the breakfast table, Aunt Fiona, and hid it in their pockets, so they knew that if they stayed up on the Guard Tower all day and all night, they'd not be hungry."

"It was still rather naughty of them," Fiona said.

"Dadda said their Tutor was a cross old man who taught them very little and was always finding fault!"

Fiona could not help thinking that it was somewhat reprehensible to tell the story to a child, but she could understand the fascination of it.

Mary-Rose looked round her, very small against the towering walls in her white gown with its blue sash.

"I wonder which is the Guard Tower," she said. "Tell me which it is, Aunt Fiona."

"We shall have to ask somebody," Fiona replied.

There appeared to be no one about and the kilted servants who had been at the entrance when they arrived were a long way away.

Then she saw in the distance the Duke come through the front door of The Castle and down the steps, followed by three dogs.

She was just wondering whether he would be annoyed to see them on the lawns, when Mary-Rose saw him too.

"There's Uncle Aiden?" she exclaimed. "He'll tell me."

Without waiting for Fiona to say anything, she sped across the grass, her fair hair glinting in the late afternoon sunshine.

For a moment the Duke, who was turning in a different direction, did not see her, then he must have heard her voice.

"Uncle Aiden! Uncle Aiden!"

She ran towards him and he turned to shout,

"Be careful of the dogs! Don't touch them!"

But it was too late.

As Fiona heard what the Duke said, she started to run, but Mary-Rose had checked her rush towards the Duke as one of the dogs moved towards her.

He was a huge mastiff, a breed Fiona had actually never seen before.

The dog suddenly stood still as if the child was something unusual and different from any human being he had seen before.

Then as the Duke called out sharply, "Rollo – come here!" Mary-Rose put out her hand to pat the dog's head.

"What a lovely dog!" she cried. "He's almost as big as me!"

It was true, Fiona thought, running now as quickly as she could, feeling that her heart was in her mouth in case the dog should savage the little girl.

The Duke must have had the same thought, for he too was moving with quick strides towards Mary-Rose.

Then both his and Fiona's paces slackened as they stared at Mary-Rose and Rollo, as if they could not believe their eyes.

The huge mastiff was wagging his tail and licking a little tentatively Mary-Rose's arms as she threw them round his neck.

As Fiona came to a standstill and drew in her breath, she realised that the Duke was also standing still and she knew by the expression on his face that he had been as afraid as she had of what might happen.

"You are the biggest and most beautiful dog I have ever seen!" Mary-Rose murmured, resting her cheek against Rollo's neck, who went on wagging his tail.

The Duke walked to Fiona's side.

"I had no idea that you would be here," he said. "I only take Rollo out when there is nobody about."

"I am sorry if we should not have been here, Your Grace, but it was a nice afternoon and I thought Mary-Rose should have some air, after being cooped up in a train for two days."

"Yes, of course," he agreed, "and quite obviously my fears for Mary-Rose where Rollo is concerned were unnecessary. But it would be wise for you to keep your distance from him."

"I am very willing to do so," Fiona said.

The Duke's eyes were still on Mary-Rose and Rollo as if he was mesmerised by the sight.

"Has she always had this power with animals?" he asked.

"I don't think it is a power, but love," Fiona replied. "She loves horses, cats, dogs and birds – in fact, everything that lives. They feel her love and respond to it."

"Is that what you believe?"

There was no mistaking the note of mockery behind the Duke's question.

Fiona looked him straight in the eyes.

"I certainly believe that love is more important than hate, Your Grace."

There was no mistaking that there was an ulterior meaning behind her words and she saw a flash of anger in the Duke's eyes.

They were both talking in low voices as if they were afraid to upset the dog and now, before the Duke could answer Fiona, Mary-Rose looked round at him, still with her arms round Rollo and asked,

"Uncle Aiden, please, can I come for a walk with you and Rollo? He's the loveliest dog I have ever seen and I think he likes me."

"That is obvious!" the Duke answered. "But perhaps you should go to bed after such a tiring journey."

"You will take me another day?" Mary-Rose asked. "Please, please, Uncle Aiden, I will be very good and I would so like to go for a walk with Rollo."

"We will see about it tomorrow."

"Thank you, Uncle Aiden."

She hugged the great mastiff again.

"I love you!" she said. "And I think you'll learn to love me. Then we will have games together."

The Duke began to walk away, followed by the other two dogs, who were the same breed but were bitches.

"Come along, Rollo," he called out.

The mastiff seemed to hesitate for a moment and then, as Mary-Rose took her arms from round his neck, he gave her another lick on her arm and bounded after his Master.

"He's the biggest dog I ever saw, Aunt Fiona!"

Fiona took the child's hand, feeling somehow shaken by the incident.

She wondered if she should tell Mary-Rose that it was unwise to touch strange dogs and then she knew that it was quite unnecessary to do so.

As she had said to the Duke, because Mary-Rose loved animals, they loved her and it was very unlikely that any of them would ever harm her.

'Why cannot we all be like that?' Fiona asked herself as they walked back towards The Castle entrance.

But she knew as she asked the question that she hated the Duke and there was no doubt that he disliked her as much as she disliked him, as he had her sister.

'If we were animals we would snarl and bite each other,' she told herself.

Then she laughed a little ruefully at the idea.

Chapter Three

Fiona had finished putting Mary-Rose to bed when Mrs. Meredith came into the room.

"Jeannie asked, miss, if you'd wish a bath before dinner."

Fiona smiled and replied,

"I would like one very much. What time will I be dining?"

As she spoke, she wondered if she would dine with the Duke or whether he would expect her, in her position as Governess, to dine alone.

"His Grace dines at eight of the clock," Mrs. Meredith replied, "and you'll be expected in the drawin' room at a quarter to the hour."

Fiona looked at the clock on the mantelpiece and saw that it was now seven o'clock.

"In which case I had better hurry."

She bent down and kissed Mary-Rose, adding,

"Good-night, my sweet. Sleep well and, if you want me, I am next door."

"I shall have lovely dreams in this big bed," Mary-Rose said, "and I expect Dadda is looking down at me and will watch over me with the angels."

"I am sure he will," Fiona answered.

She knew that her sister had taught Mary-Rose the prayer, *Four Angels Guard My Bed* and she thought whimsically as she went to her own room that the angels would certainly guard one of their own.

She wondered which dress she should wear for her first night at The Castle.

Because she felt defiant and because she had a feeling that the Duke would expect her to be crushed and subservient, she chose one of her more elaborate gowns and one with the largest bustle.

It was in fact very attractive and, although the material was not expensive, it matched the blue of her eyes and the frills that formed the bustle looked like small waves following in her wake as she walked down the passage towards the drawing room.

She thought it would be exciting tomorrow to explore The Castle with Mary-Rose.

Then as she reached the drawing room door she was sure that sooner or later the Duke would wish to speak to her about her future plans and how long she intended to stay.

'It will be a battle,' she told herself.

As a servant opened the door for her, she lifted her chin defiantly.

She somehow had expected to find the Duke alone or perhaps with Mr. McKeith, but beside him in front of a huge marble chimney piece stood a woman and another man.

They were talking as Fiona entered the room, but she was conscious of a sudden silence as she moved towards them.

As she reached the group she made a small curtsey to the Duke, saying as she did so,

"Good evening, Your Grace. I hope I am not late."

"No, Miss Windham, it is not yet eight o'clock," the Duke said, "and let me introduce you to my cousin, Lady Morag Rannock."

Fiona found herself facing a woman who was taller than herself with dark hair and distinctive features.

At first the expression in her eyes was critical and then she smiled and appeared to be friendly.

"I have just been hearing of your arrival, Miss Windham," she said, "and the Duke tells me that poor Ian's daughter is a very attractive child."

"I am sure you will think so when you meet her," Fiona replied.

"Let me introduce my other guest," the Duke interposed. "The Earl of Selway, known to me and all his friends as 'Torquil'."

The Earl, Fiona saw, was a man who, although not exactly good-looking, had a charm which she felt was somehow characteristic of the Scots – with the exception of the Duke.

At the same time she could not help feeling that the Duke not only outshone his guest but would have managed to do so however many other men were present.

He had looked resplendent when they had arrived, but in his dress kilt he was even more so, while the traditional lace cravat at his throat made him seem a little less formidable if more elegant.

His sporran was much more elaborate and in his diced hose was a jewelled *skean-dhu*, which was like the one his brother had always treasured and which at The Manor had always been laid on the table by his bed.

"I keep it near me while I sleep," he told his wife once, "so if we are attacked in the night, my darling, I will be able to defend you."

Rosemary had laughed at him for taking quite unnecessary precautions for her safety, but Fiona had guessed the real reason was that he liked looking at the memento of his Highland ancestry.

Sometimes at Christmas or on other festive occasions Ian would dress up in his kilt to please his wife and daughter.

He would tell them the history of the tartan and explain to them that it was unusual for the Lowland Scots to have a tartan or to wear the kilt.

"But the Rannocks," he explained, "were originally a Clan from the North, who fought their way to the South and settled where they are now. Their first act was to build a castle so that they could defend themselves."

He had smiled as he continued,

"They were welcome in the Lowlands because they were ferocious fighters and the Border Lairds, who were more educated and more genteel, were content to use them almost as mercenaries, to fight their battles for them."

"Surely the Rannocks were too proud to do that?" Rosemary had asked.

"The Highlanders are a warrior Society, tribal at the bottom and feudal at the top, inspired by a thousand years of legend and mythology!"

"I have always heard," Rosemary said, "and I think my father told me, that the Chieftain is the father of the Clan and there is no appeal of any sort against his authority."

"That was true," Ian had answered, "and this rule could be both tyrannous and benevolent in a minor way and, because we come from the North, my father carried on the same tradition."

There was silence as he spoke and both his wife and his sister-in-law were thinking that there had been no appeal against his father's decision to exile his recalcitrant son.

As if he knew what they were thinking, Ian went on,

"Perhaps I am fortunate. A Clanranald chief will still punish a thief by tying his hair to the seaweed on the coast, leaving him to die in the Atlantic tide and a McDonald of Sleat and a Macleod of Dunvegan would drive a hundred of their disobedient people aboard a transport ship for America."

"It sounds barbarous!" Rosemary exclaimed.

Ian smiled.

"There was also love and sacrifice in the Clan. A Highlander will cry, 'may your Chief have the ascendancy!' as a way of wishing another good fortune. By that he means that the Chieftain gives all, defends all and is all."

He went on to relate how when the Rannocks came to live in the Lowlands, although they kept their Highland traditions, they became very much more civilised.

Ian's grandfather, who had travelled abroad, spoke French and Latin as well as Gaelic and English.

"He also," Ian had added, "made a great many alterations to The Castle, making it much more comfortable."

There was a wistful expression in his eyes as he thought of his home.

Then he said,

"My father is a throwback to the Rannocks who fought the English with a fanaticism that came from the very depths of their souls. He might be forced to live on the border, but his heart remained in the original Rannock land beyond Perth. I think he missed more than anything else the wildness of the snow-capped mountains and the bleak winters that took their toll of both man and beast."

Rosemary had shivered.

"When you talk like that, darling," she said, "I am glad that I am a Sassenach and we live in England."

For once her husband did not respond and Fiona had thought that the softness of the South would never really attract him.

In some ways he was like his father and hundreds of years of Lowland life would never completely eliminate the wildness of his Northern blood.

She noticed that the Earl of Selway was wearing ordinary evening dress and she was sure that he was a

Lowland Laird. She learnt at dinner that his land marched with the Duke's land on the West.

"Once my people fought the Rannocks ferociously," he said to Fiona, "but now we live at peace with each other – at least outwardly, although I admit to often feeling an intense jealousy of my host's possessions, especially his silver."

Fiona looked at the silver ornamenting the dining room table and understood what he meant.

There were ancient goblets and cups, which she knew must have been won and treasured by the Clan for hundreds of years.

Some of them were ornamented with pale amethysts, which she knew were hewn from the mountains in some parts of Scotland, and others had garnets set in them and other semi-precious stones to which she could not put a name.

It was all very fascinating and, because she had lived a quiet, not very social life at The Manor, it was an excitement in itself to be waited on by the kilted servants and be offered delicious food served on silver dishes bearing the Rannock crest.

There was salmon, which she knew came from one of the rivers near The Castle and she wondered if the Duke was a fisherman as his brother had been.

Ian adored fishing, but because where they lived in England there were no salmon rivers, he had to content himself with catching the small speckled brown trout that Betsy would cook and which they had all enjoyed.

Sometimes Ian would talk of the salmon he had caught in his own rivers and streams and he made it sound such a thrilling pastime that Fiona could understand how much he missed it as he must miss so much of his previous life.

But his love for Rosemary had been a compensation for everything and Fiona knew that he really had no regrets, although sometimes he felt an unavoidable homesickness.

As course succeeded course, she found her hatred for the Duke rising within her until it was difficult, as she watched him sitting supreme at the head of the table, not to tell him what she thought of him.

How could he take everything for himself and never even give a thought to his brother struggling to keep his wife and child on what he was well aware was a mere pittance?

'I doubt if Ian possessed as much as he would spend in a year on the food for his dogs!' Fiona thought to herself and felt her lips tighten.

"What are you thinking about, Miss Windham?" the Earl of Selway enquired, seated beside her.

"Rather rebellious thoughts, I am afraid," Fiona answered honestly.

She was not concerned that the Duke would overhear what she was saying, because Lady Morag, who sat on his right, was making every effort to hold his attention and speaking in an intimate manner that excluded the others from joining in the conversation.

"Rebellious?" the Earl questioned. "Then be careful! The Rannocks are still very primitive and you may find yourself incarcerated in one of the dungeons or shut up at the top of a Tower from which it would be impossible for anybody to rescue you!"

"You are frightening me!" Fiona protested. "But I did feel when I arrived here that I had stepped into another world."

"I always feel the same when I come here," the Earl replied. "My castle, which I admit is very inferior to this, was only built at the beginning of the century and my father added to it in the way Prince Albert has added to Balmoral."

Fiona laughed.

"I read that His Highness had ordered a prefabricated iron ballroom which had caught his eye at the Great Exhibition."

"That is true and the grand new Baronial Hall is very impressive, but in the words of one of Her Majesty's guests – it 'still smells of paint'."

Fiona laughed again.

"The Queen really ought to live in a castle like this one."

"I can assure you that not only would the Duke not hand it over even if he was commanded to do so but he has refused several invitations to visit Balmoral."

"Why?" Fiona asked.

"He thinks the English should keep on the South side of the border!"

"Now you are really frightening me!"

She was speaking lightly. At the same time what the Earl had told her made her feel apprehensive.

'I will not leave Mary-Rose, whatever he may say,' she thought firmly.

The Earl set himself out to entertain her and he succeeded, but she would have found it difficult to talk so lightly with the Duke.

Fortunately Lady Morag made certain there was no chance of that. It was obvious that she had a very proprietary interest in her cousin.

Fiona wondered what relation she was to Mary-Rose and discovered when the ladies withdrew to the drawing room, leaving the Duke and the Earl to their port, that she was none.

Speaking in a slightly condescending manner, although Fiona thought she meant to be friendly, Lady Morag explained that she belonged to the Highland family of MacDonald, but had married a Rannock who had died.

"I had no wish to go home to my own family," she said, "so the Duke's father was kind enough to offer me accommodation in the Gate House, which has been converted into a small but charming residence."

"So you live here," Fiona said.

"It is my home," Lady Morag corrected, "and I feel now as if I was more of a Rannock than a MacDonald!"

Fiona sensed that this had something to do with her feelings for the Duke and Lady Morag continued,

"You can understand therefore how interested I shall be to meet little Mary-Rose. I have heard so much over the years of the trouble between the old Duke and his second son. Of course I knew Lord Ian when he was a boy."

"He was charming and also kind and considerate," Fiona said. "He and my sister were exceedingly happy."

"It must have been very sad for you to lose your sister in such tragic circumstances," Lady Morag remarked. "How long will you be staying here?"

"I imagine indefinitely," Fiona replied.

"Indefinitely?"

There was no mistaking the astonishment in Lady Morag's voice.

"Mary-Rose is my niece," Fiona said, "and I am all the real family she has left. As I expect you are aware, Lady Morag, the Rannocks have taken no interest in her until this particular moment"

For a moment Lady Morag did not reply.

Then she said,

"I think the Duke and most of the elderly members of the Clan will expect Mary-Rose to have a Scottish Governess, which would surely be sensible as she is to live in Scotland."

"I think as Mary-Rose grows older," Fiona said quietly, "she should have not one but several teachers. I know that many people in the Social world think that the education of women is unimportant, but my father, who was a very intelligent man, insisted that my sister, Rosemary, and I should have an extensive education equal to that of any son he might have had!"

"That sounds very advanced, Miss Windham," Lady Morag replied and Fiona suspected it was not particularly a compliment.

They were joined by the gentlemen and, as the Duke took a seat next to Lady Morag, she said,

"Miss Windham tells me, Aiden, that she expects to stay here indefinitely. I find that rather surprising."

"The length of Miss Windham's stay is something I intend to discuss with her on another occasion," the Duke answered.

Because in a way it was a snub, Fiona saw the flush that came into Lady Morag's cheeks and the manner in which she pressed her lips together.

'I must be careful,' she thought, 'I don't want to antagonise anyone, least of all a woman!'

She suddenly felt alone and rather helpless.

There was something grim and menacing about the size of The Castle and the way it seemed in her own words, 'like another world'.

It was quite a relief to see the unmistakable admiration in the Earl's eyes and to know that, because he sat as near to her as possible, he was eager to continue the conversation they had had at dinner.

"I hope it will be possible one day for you to bring Mary-Rose to see my house," he said. "I think she would be interested in my mother's aviary, which holds a great number of rare birds."

"I am sure Mary-Rose would be fascinated to see it," Fiona said enthusiastically.

"The Duke was telling me before dinner how Rollo took to her. It certainly surprises me. I had always thought him a dangerous dog to be avoided. In fact I understand he bit one of the stable boys yesterday and he now has a bad hand."

"If it is inflamed," Fiona said, "then I can do something about it."

"What do you mean by that?" the Earl enquired.

"I have quite a knowledge of herbs which I learnt from my sister and because I have found them so useful in my own life, I have brought with me to The Castle quite a number which I have picked and dried."

"That is most interesting," the Earl remarked.

He turned to the Duke, who was talking to Lady Morag, and said,

"Did you hear that, Aiden? Miss Windham has a knowledge of herbs and she says that for the wounds your ferocious animal inflicted yesterday on that wretched boy, she has something to heal them."

The Duke did not look particularly interested.

"I have sent for the local physician," he said. "Unfortunately he is away, but they expect him home the day after tomorrow."

Fiona gave a little cry.

"You should not leave a dog bite for as long as that without treatment! It can be dangerous!"

"I believe the boy is being looked after," the Duke countered.

"I assure you, unless there is somebody here who knows what he is doing, it would be easy for the boy to become seriously ill!" Fiona insisted.

The Duke looked at her with what she knew was an expression of dislike and impatience.

Then he rose from his chair and pulled at the bell that hung beside the chimney piece.

Still standing, he waited until the door opened and a servant stood awaiting his instructions,

"Fetch Mr. McKeith!" he ordered.

The servant went from the room and the Duke seated himself again.

"I have a horror of quackery of any sort," he announced, not looking at Fiona as he spoke.

"I agree with you," she said coolly. "At the same time herbs have proved efficacious all through history and the art of using them is still known to country folk not only in England but all over the world."

Lady Morag laughed.

"Of course, uneducated peasants in every country would know no better than to believe that the tongue of a toad or the hair of a cat would heal them when they have no proper sort of medicine. But then faith will move mountains!"

The Duke laughed.

"I am sure you are right there, Morag."

The door opened and Mr. McKeith came in.

He had changed into evening dress and Fiona wondered if he ate alone, having obviously not been invited to dine with the Duke.

"You wanted me, Your Grace?"

"Yes, McKeith. I wish to know how the boy Rollo bit yesterday is faring."

"I regret to tell you, Your Grace, that his hand is swollen and he is running a slight fever."

There was a silence as Mr. McKeith finished speaking and Fiona glanced at the Duke expectantly.

"Miss Windham imagines that she can help the boy with some herbs. I suppose they can do no harm until the physician can get here."

Mr. McKeith smiled.

"Mary-Rose informed me, Your Grace, that because of the efficacy of Miss Windham's herbs she was sometimes spoken of locally as a White Witch!"

Lady Morag gave a scream.

"A witch!" she exclaimed. "That is certainly something we don't like to speak about here!"

"I am certain that any witchcraft Miss Windham practises," the Earl said, "will be very harmless, unless it concerns the heart."

It was obviously a compliment and Fiona smiled as she asserted,

"I promise, Your Grace, if you will let me treat the boy, my herbs will certainly not harm him, but will take away his fever and prevent his hand from getting worse."

"Very well," the Duke agreed in an uncompromising voice. "Mr. McKeith will carry out your instructions."

"Thank you."

Fiona rose and walked quickly towards Mr. McKeith.

"Fortunately," she said as they turned to leave the room, "I have brought quite a considerable amount of herbs with me."

"If you will fetch them," Mr. McKeith said, "I will take them to the boy and get someone to apply them."

"I will do that myself."

Mr. McKeith looked surprised.

"I am sure that is unnecessary."

"If I see him, I shall be able to judge better what is best for him."

"He is sleeping above the stables," Mr. McKeith said, looking at Fiona's elegant gown.

"I will put a shawl over my shoulders, if you think he will be shocked at my not being completely covered."

She was smiling as she spoke because on their journey North they had discussed the puritanical attitude of the Scots about so many things and Mr. McKeith had told her how many of the older people were horrified at the thought of men and women going about 'half-naked'.

"I will wait for you in the hall," Mr. McKeith said, as if he capitulated in regard to her determination to attend the boy herself.

Fiona ran to her room.

She had treated dog bites before and Rosemary had taught her that *Hercules Wound-Wort*, which the people in the village near The Manor called *All Heal*, was excellent for the bites of mad dogs and verminous beasts.

Rollo was not mad, but, if his teeth had drawn blood, the wounds might easily turn septic and it sounded, since the boy had a fever, as if that had already happened.

She had packed in her luggage a case that contained many packets of herbs and some lotions and elixirs that Rosemary had taught her to distil all through the year as the required herbs became available.

Opening a case, Fiona found a packet of *All Heal*, which she wanted the boy to take and also one of borage, which would remove the fever.

She decided that *Alkenet*, which was a common herb in Kent, would be best to apply to the wounds. She always kept a pot of it made into a cream so that she could use it on Mary-Rose if ever she fell and bruised herself.

With the three herbs in her hand, she ran back along the corridor and down the stairs to where she found Mr. McKeith waiting for her.

Beside him was Donald, the resplendent Major Do-mo who had greeted them on their arrival.

"The boy who is injured, Miss Windham, is Donald's grandson!" Mr. McKeith explained.

"It's verra kind of you, miss, to trouble yoursel for the lad," Donald said. "He's a good boy and first rate with the horses and His Grace's sportin' dogs, but Rollo can be nasty at times and it's my opinion he should have been put down a long time since."

"I agree with you, Donald," Mr. McKeith said, "but His Grace is fond of the animal."

Fiona found it difficult to speak when she thought of what might have happened to Mary-Rose this evening had the dog savaged her.

When she saw the damage done to the boy's hand, she was inclined to agree with Donald and Mr. McKeith that the dog should be put away.

Malcolm, the boy who had been bitten, was large for his age, but not yet a grown man and he was, Fiona knew, being brave, despite the fact that his hand had been badly mauled and the inflammation was rising up his arm.

His father, who was a groom, his mother and her other four children were all with him and they were packed into what seemed to Fiona to be a very small space above the stables.

However, the place was spotlessly clean and Malcolm's mother appeared to understand exactly what Fiona told her about soaking and mixing the herbs and how often her son was to take them.

The potion smelt rather nasty and it had not a particularly pleasant taste, but Malcolm, somewhat overcome at the presence of Fiona and Mr. McKeith, drank it manfully and promised to take it every four hours.

Fiona then applied the cream to his wounds and bound them skilfully in a manner that made Mr. McKeith say,

"I can see, Miss Windham, that you have had a great deal of practice."

"My sister was famous in the countryside for the help she would give to everybody. There would sometimes be a dozen patients waiting to see her in the morning."

She smiled as she added,

"There would be men who had cut their hands on a scythe or a saw, small boys who had fallen out of trees and women with babies who had strange complaints for which the doctor could give nothing more efficacious than bread pills and the advice not to worry."

As Mr. McKeith laughed, Fiona added,

"That always meant, we knew, that he had not the slightest idea what was the matter with them."

Fiona finished bandaging Malcolm and told him,

"You will soon be better and I think you will find that by tomorrow morning the fever will have left you."

"It be awful kind of you, miss."

She and Mr. McKeith walked back to The Castle and now it was dark. The stars shone overhead and looking up Fiona could see the statues on the towers silhouetted against the sky.

"It is beautiful, but awe-inspiring!" she said aloud.

"After a time you will have a feeling of protection, of being immunised from the troubles of the ordinary world outside."

"If that happens, it sounds very pleasing," Fiona replied.

She thought as she spoke that she might not stay long enough to reach this enviable phase and she wondered when the Duke would talk to her as he had said he intended to do.

She did not have to wait long to find out.

It had taken some time to prepare the herbs and to apply them and, when she and Mr. McKeith walked up the stone staircase towards the drawing room, they met the Earl and Lady Morag halfway down the stairs.

"We wondered what had happened to you," the Earl said to Fiona.

"My patient needed quite a good deal of attention," she replied.

"I hope he is grateful."

"He will be!" Fiona replied confidently.

"If he recovers I shall be quite frightened!" Lady Morag said. "Quite frankly, witchcraft terrifies me! What do you think, Torquil?"

He did not reply and Fiona thought that it would be undignified to tell her that she was talking nonsense and, as she and Mr. McKeith stood aside, Lady Morag and the Earl continued to descend the stairs.

"I am taking Lady Morag home," the Earl said to Fiona, as if he wished to explain his actions. "I shall see you tomorrow and may I say I am already looking forward to making the acquaintance of Mary-Rose."

Fiona smiled at him.

Then, as if it was difficult to tear himself away, he hurried after Lady Morag.

She could not understand why, but, as they went up the stairs Fiona felt that Mr. McKeith found Lady Morag a tiresome woman.

It would, however, have been wrong to comment on a relative of the Duke's and they reached the drawing room in silence.

"Perhaps His Grace has also retired to bed," she said, hoping that he had done so.

"That is unlikely," Mr. McKeith replied, "and we must, of course, report progress."

"I suppose so," Fiona agreed with a sigh.

She felt a little tired.

It had been a long day and, despite the comfort of her bed in the train, she had not slept particularly well.

This, she knew, was because she was nervous of what lay ahead and worried about her own future as well as that of Mary-Rose.

It was one thing to decide to fight, but it was quite a different one to approach the battle cold-bloodedly.

Now, as they entered the drawing room, she saw that Mr. McKeith had been right in assuming that the Duke would not have retired to bed.

He was standing up in his favourite position in front of the chimney piece, holding an open newspaper in his hands.

He put it down as they advanced towards him and, when they had nearly reached him, he asked sharply,

"Well?"

"The boy was rather worse than when I saw him earlier in the day, Your Grace," Mr. McKeith said. "His wrist and the lower part of his arm are badly swollen."

The Duke looked at Fiona.

"Is there anything you can do?"

As he asked the question, she was certain that he would expect her to admit her incompetence.

"I have given him herbs, Your Grace, to take away both the fever and any poison that has infected the bite. I have also bandaged his arm, using a cream that I have never known to fail in such circumstances."

"You sound as if you are experienced in this sort of work."

"I have helped my sister for the last three years and we have seldom had a failure."

"You surprise me," the Duke commented drily,

He looked at Mr. McKeith.

"I think that will be all for this evening, McKeith."

"I thank Your Grace. Goodnight!"

"Goodnight!" the Duke said.

Fiona knew, as Mr. McKeith walked towards the drawing room door, that the interview she had dreaded was upon her.

She was aware that she must have all her wits about her and try not to antagonise the Duke to the point of turning her out of The Castle.

'I must think of Mary-Rose and that her interests are all that matters,' Fiona thought.

Then, as the door closed behind Mr. McKeith, she lifted her chin and waited.

"Perhaps you should sit down, Miss Windham," the Duke suggested.

"If I do, I hope Your Grace will do the same."

He looked surprised.

"You are so tall," Fiona explained, "that I shall feel even before you speak that you are overpowering me."

"Is that what you are expecting me to do?"

"I am afraid so, but let me add that I am far from being ready to capitulate, before or after a shot has been fired!"

There was a faint twist of his lips as the Duke enquired,

"Are you telling me, Miss Windham, that you intend to do battle?"

"But of course!" Fiona replied.

"There really does not seem to be any reason for us to be at loggerheads," the Duke said.

"I should have thought that Mary-Rose was a very good reason. She is, as far as I am concerned."

"I am sure Mr. McKeith explained to you that as my heir-presumptive it is right and proper that Mary-Rose should live here amongst her father's people."

"Even though her father was exiled from them?" Fiona enquired.

"That is past history."

"My brother-in-law was alive until a year ago. He made the home where he lived with my sister and Mary-

Rose a very happy one. I intend to look after my niece and make her life as happy and complete as possible, even though she no longer has a father and mother."

"I am sure that is very commendable on your part, Miss Windham, but you are a young woman and you will doubtless wish to marry."

"That is unlikely, but even if I did find a man who could make me as happy as your brother made my sister, there would always be a place, wherever I lived, for my niece."

"Her place is here! She is a Rannock and must be brought up to understand her future responsibilities."

"I think if Mary-Rose understood what those responsibilities did to her father, she would not be as thrilled by The Castle or at meeting you as she is now."

There was silence for a moment and then the Duke said,

"Am I to believe that Mary-Rose has no idea that her father was not welcome here?"

"Of course she has no idea of that!" Fiona replied sharply. "Ian was loyal, completely loyal, to you and to his father. He never said anything derogatory about you nor did he ever complain of the treatment he received because he married someone he loved."

She drew in her breath and then could not prevent herself from going on,

"When I see the style in which you live and when I remember how Ian had to count every penny he spent, I find it very difficult to believe that Mary-Rose would be happy here, amongst people who are not only insensitive but cruel!"

"I imagine you are referring particularly to me," the Duke remarked.

"That is for you to judge," Fiona replied.

Her words had inevitably aroused her temper and now she stared at the Duke, her large eyes aflame with anger.

There was a silence before the Duke said,

"As your own feelings towards me are very obvious, Miss Windham, can I really believe that you are the right person to teach Mary-Rose the tolerance and understanding she will need to deal with our Clan?"

Fiona did not speak and after a moment he went on,

"I expect your brother-in-law told you that the Rannocks are different from any other Scots in this part of the world. We are Highlanders and because of it we keep ourselves very much to ourselves, almost as if we were living in a foreign country."

He paused before he continued,

"Our feelings, our beliefs and our traditions are those which we acquired in the North and because we are a close-knit community our people look to their Chieftain for guidance as other Scots have forgotten to do."

"Ian explained that to me," Fiona said, "and I think, because Mary-Rose is a very exceptional child and has a sympathy and understanding of people far beyond her years, she will grow up into an exceptional woman."

"That is what I hope, but you will understand, Miss Windham, that I consider it necessary for her at her age to be taught by those who know our peculiarities and, perhaps, our limitations."

"I know exactly what you are trying to say to me, Your Grace. You wish me to leave Mary-Rose here."

"Not immediately," the Duke interposed, "but as soon as she is acclimatised to The Castle and has met a number of her relations who live in the vicinity or who would come down from the North to meet her."

"Let me make one thing quite clear from the very beginning," Fiona said. "I do not intend to leave Mary-Rose alone with you."

The Duke stiffened and she knew that the resolute way in which she had spoken had surprised him.

He rose from his chair to stand once again with his back to the chimney piece, as if it gave him support.

"I have no wish to cross swords with you at this moment, Miss Windham," he said, "but what you are suggesting is most impractical."

"Why?"

"I can give you the answer to that in one word – you are English!"

"Why not say a Sassenach? A description which, amongst others, your father used to insult my sister!"

The Duke raised his eyebrows.

"In case you did not see the letter that he wrote to his son when he had told him he had fallen in love and wished to marry," Fiona said in an icy voice, "His Grace wrote that he forbade Ian to marry – a woman who was a Sassenach, an actress and doubtless a prostitute!"

The Duke started.

"I had no idea that my father had been so forceful, but my brother's desertion, which was how he saw it, affected him very deeply."

"Ian was a very wonderful person," Fiona said. "He knew what his father's reaction would be to his marriage, but he believed that any sacrifice was worthwhile where my sister was concerned,"

She drew in her breath before she continued,

"But he hoped and believed that you were not so bigoted and that the companionship and the love you had for each other when you were boys would free you from such prejudiced intolerance."

Fiona spoke passionately and she realised as she clenched her fingers together that she was trembling with the intensity of her feelings.

Then, before the Duke could speak, she said,

"I don't wish to antagonise you, since I intend to stay here with Mary-Rose, but it is difficult to speak calmly when I remember how much you hurt your brother."

Again there was silence, as the Duke stared ahead of him with unseeing eyes.

'I have said too much,' Fiona thought to herself. 'Now I shall have to go. He will insist upon it.'

She could hear the clock on the mantelpiece ticking and thought that it was like the beat of her heart, which seemed to have moved into her throat.

Still the Duke did not speak, until finally, in words that seemed slow, almost as if he considered each one before it came to his lips, he said,

"I think, Miss Windham, we should leave this discussion for the moment. It would be easy for both of us to say things which we might afterwards regret and what must be uppermost in both our minds is, of course, what is best for Mary-Rose."

"That is all I want you to consider."

"Shall I promise you it is what I *will* consider?" the Duke asked. "But recriminations will get us nowhere."

That was true, Fiona knew.

At the same time she knew that there was so much more she wanted to say.

Then she told herself that he was being sensible and she was being emotional.

She rose from the chair where she had been sitting.

"I apologise to Your Grace," she said in a low voice, "if I have been too rude. If you think it was an impertinence, I can only ask you to forgive me – because I loved your brother so deeply and I miss him – as I miss my sister – every moment of the day."

In spite of her resolution, Fiona heard her voice break a little on the words and in case the Duke should see that there were tears in her eyes, she curtseyed with her eyes downcast and her eyelashes dark against her cheeks.

"Goodnight – Your Grace."

Her voice was so low that it was barely above a whisper.

"Goodnight, Miss Windham."

Fiona walked away and it seemed a long way to the door.

She thought imaginatively that she could almost feel his eyes boring into her back.

Chapter Four

Mary-Rose lay down after luncheon and Fiona wandered downstairs and out the front door.

She passed through the courtyard and onto the grass that surrounded The Castle inside the great high walls.

It was a lovely day with bright sunshine and a touch of wind. Fiona felt her hair being whipped against her cheeks and was somehow glad of its roughness.

Ever since arriving in Scotland she had had the feeling of being incarcerated almost like a prisoner, but the wind made her feel that outside there was the freshness of the air and the wildness of the countryside and freedom.

Mary-Rose had been tired after the journey and at first Fiona had allowed her to play only within the confines of The Castle itself, then yesterday and this morning they had taken a short walk.

Fiona had been thrilled to see the Scottish landscape undulating away towards the fir-clad hills in the distance.

Today there was no mist on them and they stood like sentinels against the sky. She fancied that she could see several silver cascades such as her brother-in-law had always told her were an intrinsic part of the Scottish scenery.

She and Mary-Rose walked for a little while beside a small stream, trying to see if there were any fish beneath its clear surface, but Fiona had learnt that the main river where the salmon were caught was nearly a mile away.

"We will go there as soon as you feel your legs are strong enough to carry you," she promised Mary-Rose.

"I want to catch a big fish like Dadda did when he was my age."

"We shall have to talk to your uncle about that," Fiona replied. "I am sure you could have a small rod and learn how to fish."

She knew that the child was excited at the idea and she told herself that she would speak to the Duke about it that evening at dinner.

It was in fact the only time she saw him.

In the daytime he went riding, as he had done this morning, with the Earl.

Fiona, watching them trot away towards the middle gate, had thought how well the Duke rode and how distinguished he looked on a horse, wearing not the kilt but the more convenient tartan trews as his ancestors had for hundreds of years.

The horse the Duke was riding was very spirited, but he handled it with an unmistakable expertise.

Then Fiona remembered the inferior, cheap animals, which were all that his brother Ian had been able to ride and she thought once again how much she hated the Duke for his selfishness and indifference towards someone who had loved him ever since they had been children together.

And she thought, as she had thought a thousand times since she had come to The Castle, how unfair it was that the oldest son should always take everything.

Then a voice behind her made her start.

"I somehow expected you to be out enjoying the sunshine, Miss Windham."

She turned to find that the Earl had approached without her hearing him and she looked at him in surprise.

"I thought you were riding with His Grace," she replied.

"I was," the Earl answered, "but my horse went lame, so Aiden went on without me."

"Where were you going?" Fiona enquired curiously.

"To one of the outlying parts of the Rannock estate," the Earl replied. "Aiden wanted to see how his tartan weavers were progressing."

"Tartan weavers?" Fiona questioned.

"I expected you to know that the Duke has solved quite a lot of local unemployment," the Earl explained, "by setting up small industries in a number of hamlets, so that the Clan can become almost self-supporting and provide themselves with everything they need from their own land."

"I did not know that," Fiona replied. "But it is certainly a good idea!"

"An excellent one and something I intend to copy in my own part of the country," the Earl smiled.

As they walked slowly across the soft green grass, Fiona said a little tentatively,

"I am glad to hear that he has other interests outside The Castle. I was beginning to feel that the Duke lived a very isolated existence and in consequence I am rather worried about Mary-Rose."

There was silence and she added,

"I am not meaning to be critical, but I have been here a week and there have been no visitors except for yourself and, of course, Lady Morag. I always thought Ducal houses were a hive of entertainment and hospitality."

Again there was silence and, as she looked at the Earl, he said slowly,

"I thought, of course, that on your way here from the South Mr. McKeith would have explained the situation to you."

"What situation?"

She thought that the Earl looked at her in surprise before he asked,

"You have no idea?"

"Frankly, I don't know what you are talking about."

"Then perhaps I had better tell you," he suggested, "although it is slightly embarrassing for me."

"Tell me what?" Fiona asked.

"Why my friend Aiden has no visitors and why, as you say, The Castle seems very isolated."

"I thought there must be neighbours somewhere in the vicinity," Fiona murmured.

"There are," the Earl agreed. "In this part of the country there are a great number of houses and castles occupied by influential lowland families, like the Hamiltons, the Bruces, and the Ogilvys, all of them only too willing to be hospitable to me."

He smiled a little wryly as he added,

"In fact, often I have more invitations than I can possibly accept."

This did not surprise Fiona, who found the Earl charming and at times very amusing.

"Then why – ?" she began.

"Aiden is in a different category."

"Because he is so aloof and in a way repressive?"

The Earl shook his head.

"No, it is nothing like that. Aiden was one of the most charming and delightful boys imaginable. His brother was very like him, although, of course, Ian being younger than he was, I did not see so much of him."

"Then why did he change?" Fiona enquired.

"His marriage did that to him. Ian must have told you how desperately unhappy he was. Janet MacDonald was in fact a fiend in human form."

"MacDonald?" Fiona exclaimed. "Then she was related to Lady Morag."

"Her younger sister. Did you not know that?"

"The Duke introduced her as his cousin. Why did he not say that she is his sister-in-law?"

"He never refers to his wife if he can help it and in fact Lady Morag was married to his cousin."

"Please tell me everything I should know," Fiona pleaded, "so that I will not make any silly mistakes."

"I am beginning to wish I had not got myself into this," the Earl said a little ruefully.

"Please tell me," Fiona begged. "Having said so much, you cannot leave me in ignorance."

"No, I see that and anyway I think it is right that you should know."

The Earl seemed almost to fortify himself before he began,

"Aiden married Janet MacDonald, a marriage arranged by the old Duke and the Chief of the MacDonalds, but if ever two people were incompatible, it was they!"

"I have always thought that arranged marriages were barbarous," Fiona murmured.

"I agree with you, but Aiden's marriage was connected with Rannock lands in the North and the old Duke considered that nothing else was of any importance."

"So they were unhappy?"

"Aiden was utterly and completely miserable and with reason, for I don't think Janet was at all normal in many ways. At any rate she made his life a hell until she disappeared."

"How did she do that?"

"That is what no one has been able to discover," the Earl replied.

"Mr. McKeith told me there had been an intensive search and they had followed up every possible clue."

"That is true, but what he omitted to tell you was that Aiden is suspected of being responsible."

Fiona stood still and stared at him wide-eyed.

"Are you saying that people suspect the Duke of – having murdered the Duchess?"

"No one has been brave enough to put it so bluntly, at least not to him. But to be truthful, suspicion has grown over the years until I think I am right in saying that the majority of those who live in these parts think that Aiden murdered Janet in a fit of rage and then somehow disposed of her body."

The Earl did not speak for a moment and Fiona commented,

"I have hated the Duke for the way he treated his brother, but I find it hard to believe that he is a murderer."

"I am glad to hear you say that, Miss Windham, and I am completely and absolutely convinced in my own mind that it would be alien to every instinct in Aiden's body to kill anyone in cold blood, especially a woman."

"You believe in him," Fiona said quietly. "Is that why you are here?"

"Aiden is my oldest friend," the Earl answered, "and because I know what a lonely life he leads and because I think, although we have never discussed it, that he is aware of what people think about him, I come here to be with him whenever I can spare the time."

"That is kind of you."

"Not really. He is a man I like and admire and I am extremely happy in his company."

The Earl spoke almost aggressively, as if he defied her to think otherwise.

Fiona drew in her breath.

"I cannot believe that what the Duke is suspected of could possibly be true. Surely somebody can find out what happened to the Duchess?"

The Earl spread out his hands in a gesture of help-lessness.

"One day she was there – the next day she had vanished! Nobody saw her leave. Nobody has found any trace of her here or in the surrounding countryside. The whole scenario is a complete mystery."

"A very horrible one, especially if the Duke is innocent."

"He *is* innocent," the Earl said positively. "I would stake my life on it, but God knows how I can ever prove it."

"Now I understand," Fiona said quietly, almost as if she was talking to herself, "why he seems so aloof, why he appears at times to deliberately stand aside from life and regard it cynically."

She was putting her thoughts into words and the Earl exclaimed,

"That is intelligent and perceptive of you. Of course Aiden stands apart from life when he knows what people are thinking and cannot challenge them because they will never dare to put their thoughts into words."

He sighed before he continued,

"At first he was hopeful that they would find the Duchess, but now I believe he has given up hope and has resigned himself to a life of loneliness, isolated from his neighbours, and surrounded by an atmosphere of suspicion which he feels infects even the most loyal of his followers."

Fiona was silent.

What the Earl had just told her made her see the Duke in a very different perspective from how she had seen him before.

"What about his relatives?" she questioned aloud.

"Most of them live on Rannock lands in the North," the Earl replied. "They have extremely plausible excuses as to why they should not accept Aiden's invitations to stay here."

His voice was sceptical as he added,

"They are all Doubting Thomases, with the exception, of course, of Lady Morag."

Fiona had known, from the way the Earl spoke and the way he had looked at Lady Morag when she came to dinner, that he disliked her.

Now she asked a little hesitatingly, because she did not wish to appear too curious,

"Why does – Lady Morag stay on? She must find it – lonely as well."

"Not while the Duke is here," the Earl replied. "You cannot be so obtuse as not to realise where her interest lies."

Lady Morag made it very obvious, Fiona thought, that she was pursuing the Duke, and when she came to dinner she monopolised him in a manner that was in fact extremely impolite towards everyone else present.

Fiona was also woman enough to be aware of the hunger in her eyes when she looked at the Duke and she thought that the manner in which Lady Morag was, if not rude, then condescending and crushing towards her might be accounted for by the fact that she was jealous.

Now she remarked aloud,

"At least she has been loyal."

"To suit her own ends," the Earl said drily.

Fiona thought that he was perhaps being a little unfair. At the same time she had no reason to stand up for Lady Morag.

When the stable boy, Angus, had been much better the morning after she had treated his swollen arm and was back at work within three days, Lady Morag had made a great fuss about it being witchcraft.

"The Clan will not like it!" she had said to the Duke in Fiona's hearing. "The Scots have always had a horror of witches, as you well know."

"You can hardly describe Miss Windham as a witch!" the Duke objected.

"You can be a witch without looking like one," Lady Morag retorted, "and magic herbs are always the tools of the trade."

"People who are intelligent," Fiona had said, feeling that she must defend herself, "know that nature provides the antidote to every ill, like the nettle and the dock leaf. The country folk in England know a great deal about the healing powers of herbs."

Lady Morag shivered in an exaggerated fashion.

"It all seems very creepy to me," she said, "and personally I prefer to rely on a physician."

That should have been the end of the matter, but Fiona suspected that Lady Morag was talking of her using witchcraft not only to the Duke but to the servants at The Castle.

She remembered reading that the Scottish witch-hunts in the seventeenth and eighteenth centuries had resulted in four thousand poor old women being convicted as witches and burned at the stake.

As there had been only half that number of victims in England, despite the size of the population, she was well aware that the Scots could be fanatical on the subject.

Yet she told herself that for Mary-Rose's sake she must be tactful and not attack Lady Morag for trying to make trouble.

Equally she told herself that such foolish and ill-advised talk could be dangerous and should not be encouraged.

Now she found herself wondering what sort of life it must be for the Duke to have so few friends, so few people round him who believed in his integrity.

Because he was so proud and so autocratic, the situation was perhaps more bitter and more hurting than it might have been to somebody of a different character.

'If he knows in his heart that he is innocent,' Fiona thought to herself, 'it must be desperately frustrating to know that he is whispered about behind his back, ostracised without anyone saying so, while there is nothing he can do about it.'

It struck her that perhaps this was the reason why he had not been in touch with his brother after the old Duke's death.

Then she thought he must have known that whatever had happened, whether he had or had not actually committed a crime, Ian would have stood by him and supported him in every possible way.

'Why did he not give him the chance?' Fiona wondered, but she could find no answer.

"Now let's talk about you," the Earl said unexpectedly.

"Me?" Fiona questioned. "But why?"

"I can think of no subject more fascinating!"

The look in the Earl's eyes was more eloquent than his words.

"I must go – back," Fiona said quickly. "It is time for me to awaken Mary-Rose and give her a music lesson."

"I am sure the child is peacefully asleep," the Earl said, "and therefore does not need you, while I do."

"You have forgotten, my Lord, that I am here in the capacity of a Governess."

"May I say in all sincerity that you certainly don't look like one," the Earl replied. "Indeed, you are so beautiful that I am beginning to think you are in fact the witch that Lady Morag believes you to be!"

"You are not to say that!" Fiona scolded him sharply.

"How can I help it when you bewitch me?"

"I think, my Lord, that you are trying to flirt with me and that is something which must not happen here. As you are well aware, the Duke would welcome any excuse to send me away from Mary-Rose and that is something I have no intention of allowing him to do."

"Actually I am not flirting," the Earl said.

Now there was a deep note in his voice and an expression in his eyes that frightened Fiona.

"Please – please," she insisted, "don't say any more. I am in a very difficult position and, as I have no wish to leave Mary-Rose alone amongst all these dour Scots, I have to tread warily."

"I understand what you are saying," the Earl replied, "of course I do! But it's difficult for me ever to see you alone and there is so much I want to tell you, so much I want to say."

"But you must not say it," Fiona said quickly. "Please be careful! I know it is dangerous for you to show any interest in me as a woman."

"As I have eyes in my head and a heart in my body can you expect me to do anything else? God in Heaven! I never expected in my wildest dreams to find anyone so beautiful surrounded by the walls of Rannock Castle!"

The way he spoke made Fiona give a little laugh.

Then, as they reached the entrance to the courtyard, they both saw to their surprise a familiar figure coming down the steps from the front door.

It was the Duke and he had changed from the tartan trews he had worn while riding, into his kilt.

He walked towards them, looking extremely handsome and at the same time so overpowering that Fiona felt almost guilty, as if she had been caught committing some indiscretion.

"You are back very early, Aiden!" the Earl exclaimed.

"When you left me, I decided it was too far to go on alone," the Duke replied, "so I followed you home."

"I have been telling Miss Windham how my horse went lame."

Fiona saw the Duke glance first at the Earl, then at her and she could read without words the suspicion in his mind.

"I must go and wake Mary-Rose, Your Grace. She has been resting," she said and quickly walked past him to enter The Castle.

She ran up the front stairs as if there were somebody after her, aware that she was in fact feeling very uncomfortable because of what she sensed the Duke was thinking.

'I have done nothing wrong,' she told herself, 'and my private life is my own.'

At the same time, because she loved Mary-Rose, she was afraid.

The child was still asleep when Fiona went into her room, so she walked into the sitting room that had been arranged opposite their two bedrooms.

It was a large and pleasant room and Mr. McKeith had provided it with a piano which was Mary-Rose's delight.

She already played extremely well for a child of her age, which was not surprising as her mother had been such an exceptional musician.

Fiona enjoyed playing, but she had none of her sister's genius.

Music could bring her tranquillity when she was upset and was an escape from anything that made her feel apprehensive.

She sat down now at the piano and began to play softly, trying to ease away the little constriction in her heart that she knew was in reality a touch of fear.

'It is absurd for me to be afraid of anybody,' she told herself and thought it was something that she had never felt in the past.

But the Duke was certainly awe-inspiring and what really made her fearful was the knowledge that suddenly she might be ordered to leave The Castle and go South.

Even before she had learnt what the Earl had just told her about the Duke, she had thought that she could not desert Mary-Rose and now it seemed even more impossible.

What sort of life would the child have there without friends and without companions of her own age?

Fiona remembered now how Ian had told her that, when he was young, there had always been all sorts of interests that they shared with their neighbours.

There had been Highland games and gymkhanas and shooting parties over the moors, besides the English game of cricket.

Ian told her that his brother Aiden had been an extremely competent bowler.

"We used to beat all the local teams!" he had said boastfully.

How could Mary-Rose grow up seeing nobody but her uncle, Lady Morag and occasionally the Earl?

It was an impossible situation, but Fiona was not quite certain what she could do about it.

*

That evening she broached the subject of Mary-Rose learning to fish.

"She has been told by Donald how he helped her father to catch his first fish when he was her age," she said. "Perhaps it would be possible for her to have lessons with a light trout rod."

"I imagine the rod both Ian and I used is somewhere in The Castle," the Duke replied.

"Then can Donald take her to the river?" Fiona enquired.

Lady Morag, who was dining with them, interposed,

"Personally, I think Mary-Rose is much too young, Aiden, and besides, fishing is a boy's pursuit. Surely Miss

Windham can find something more feminine for her to do?"

Fiona's lips tightened.

She had an idea that Lady Morag was being obstructive only because fishing was something that she had suggested.

"I see no reason why Mary-Rose should not be taught to fish," the Duke said after a moment. "Unless I am mistaken, she will soon find it boring unless she catches something."

"She will be very lucky if she does that!" the Earl exclaimed. "I fished for three hours yesterday without a single rise."

"You were unlucky," the Duke laughed.

"That is what I want to believe," the Earl replied, "but I have an uncomfortable feeling that the reason you caught two salmon in the same amount of time is that you are more skilful."

"I think actually it is because I know these waters better," the Duke smiled.

For once he looked quite human.

Then the smile faded and he said,

"You can tell McKeith, Miss Windham, that Mary-Rose can go fishing with Donald."

"And may I go too, Your Grace? As it happens, your brother taught me to fish for trout and it is something I greatly enjoy."

"Oh, really, Miss Windham!" Lady Morag exclaimed before the Duke could speak. "There is no end to your versatilities and such unexpected ones! First you are a witch with herbs, now you are a fisherman and, as I understand it, you are quite skilful at the piano as your sister was. But she, of course, was a professional performer."

There was no doubt that Lady Morag intended to be unpleasant and it was with difficulty that Fiona managed to say in a deliberately sweet voice,

"How very kind of you to be so flattering!"

She heard the Earl give a little choke of laughter beside her and she thought that perhaps she should not have answered at all.

Then, as she met Lady Morag's eyes, she knew that she had made an implacable enemy and it would be wise to be on her guard.

Because she had no wish to make things worse than they were already, as soon as she and Lady Morag left the dining room, Fiona made some excuse to retire, knowing that the older woman was only too delighted to see her go.

She peeped into Mary-Rose's room to see if she was asleep and then went into the sitting room.

She wanted to play the piano, but she thought that it might be a mistake in case the sound was overheard, for it would seem rude to have left the Duke's presence for any reason except that she had retired to bed.

She found a book that interested her and sat for a while reading it, then went to her bedroom.

She undressed and, after continuing to read for some time, blew out the candles and closed her eyes.

She was almost asleep when there was a soft knock on her door.

For a moment Fiona thought she must have imagined it and then the knock came again.

She sat up in bed, feeling for the matches.

The main rooms of The Castle were lit by lamps, but candles were used in the bedrooms and Fiona liked their soft, gentle, romantic light instead of the hardness of gas, which they had used at The Manor.

"Come in!" she called out.

The door opened as she lit the first candle and then she saw Mrs. Meredith.

"I'm real sorry to disturb you, miss," she said apologetically, "but Jeannie's awful bad and I thought you might be able to help her."

"Jeannie?" Fiona exclaimed, sitting up in bed. "I wondered why she did not attend Miss Mary-Rose this evening."

"She complained of having a wee cold yesterday," Mrs. Meredith explained, "but this mornin' she was almost speechless and now she has a fever."

"I'll come and see her," Fiona said.

"'Tis very kind of you, miss, and I don't like to give you any trouble."

"It's no trouble at all, Mrs. Meredith," Fiona reassured her. "Just give me a minute to find the herbs I want. Or better still, go back to Jeannie. Tell me where she sleeps."

"Go straight to the end of the corridor, miss, and you'll find a staircase which'll lead you up to the next floor. I'll listen for you."

Having spoken, Mrs. Meredith paused.

"'Tis not right, I shouldna be a-botherin' you with comin' up to Jeannie's room at this time of night. Let me come back for the herbs when you've found them, miss."

"No, I would rather bring them myself," Fiona answered. "If you want to help, you can boil a kettle of water, which will make it easier for me to treat Jeannie as quickly as possible."

"I'll do that, miss, and thank you."

Mrs. Meredith hurried away, shutting the door behind her. Fiona climbed out of bed to find her case, which contained the herbs and she chose those which she thought would be suitable to treat a fever that had obviously started with a head cold.

She could not be certain until she had seen Jeannie and taken her temperature exactly which herbs would be the most efficacious, so she chose several packets.

Then, slipping on a dressing gown that was of blue silk to match her eyes, Fiona opened the door to the passage and saw with relief that the candles in the huge silver sconces that bore the Duke's crest were still alight.

The passage was covered with the Rannock tartan as a carpet and, as soon as Fiona had passed what she knew were the main rooms of the house, one of which was occupied by the Earl, it became narrower.

Fiona circumnavigated the curve of the walls and went on into what she knew was the oldest part of The Castle, which had not been renovated.

She found the narrow twisting staircase that led up to the next floor and, when she reached the top of it, Mrs. Meredith was waiting for her.

Jeannie was in a small but comfortable bedroom and Fiona saw at once that she had a high fever.

It was almost impossible for her to speak and her eyes were so bright that it was difficult to know if she recognised anybody.

Mrs. Meredith had the kettle ready and, when Fiona had mixed two powerful herbs together, the housekeeper lifted Jeannie up in her arms so that Fiona could persuade her to drink it.

When they laid her down again, she muttered something incoherent and snuggled down against the pillows.

"She will go to sleep and may not wake for many hours," Fiona said in a low voice. "I will come and see her in the morning. By then I expect the fever will have broken."

"'Tis wonderful what you can do, miss, with stuff that looks like nothin' more than bits of grass," Mrs. Meredith said admiringly.

"It's the herbs that are wonderful," Fiona answered. "God gave them to us, but we don't always have the intelligence to use them."

"That's true enough, miss. I was rememberin' just now that my mother used to believe in dandelion wine when she was feelin' poorly."

"I am sure Jeannie will be better in the morning," Fiona said. "Go to bed and don't worry. I very much doubt if she will wake up and disturb you."

"I'm ever so grateful – I am indeed, miss," Mrs. Meredith said.

Fiona smiled at her and started to descend the staircase.

As she reached the passage, she saw that, since she had gone up to the next floor nearly all the candles had been extinguished.

There were, however, two or three left at the far end where her bedroom was situated and it was therefore not difficult for her to find her way towards the light.

She was walking along, not hurrying but thinking of Jeannie and hoping that she would recover quickly, when suddenly at the other end of the passage she saw a tall figure.

For a moment, because there was so little light, it was difficult to distinguish who it was and yet with a frightened leap of her heart Fiona guessed who it was.

She did not slacken or accelerate her pace and only when she had progressed quite a bit farther down the passage was she sure that it was the Duke she could see ahead, but for the moment he had not seen her.

Then, as she wondered whether it would be better to hide in the shadows of a doorway or continue to advance, she was aware that he was looking at her.

In that second she suddenly became self-conscious, knowing how strange she must look in her floating blue robe with her fair hair hanging loose over her shoulders.

'Perhaps he will think it unconventional for me to concern myself with one of the housemaids so late at night,' she thought.

Then a second later she came within a few feet of him and unless he stood aside to let her pass it would be impossible for her to proceed.

She looked up at him and could see, or thought she could in the indistinct light, that he was angry.

It was impossible to walk on and they faced each other squarely on the tartan carpet, Fiona feeling that in contrast to herself, the Duke, in his evening kilt, elaborate sporran and lace jabot at his throat, looked overwhelmingly resplendent.

'He must be wondering what I have been doing,' she thought, but before she could say anything he spoke first,

"Where have you been, Miss Windham?"

He spoke so harshly, indeed roughly, that she was startled.

Everything she had been about to say seemed to go out of her head.

"I have – " she began and thought that her voice seemed thin and rather incoherent.

Then the Duke interposed,

"Don't bother to lie! The answer to my question is obvious! I thought you were different!"

Fiona lifted her head to look up at him questioningly.

"I – don't – " she began again.

But now the Duke asked furiously in a voice that seemed to vibrate with anger,

"Have you had enough lovemaking for tonight or are you looking for more?"

As he spoke, to her astonishment in one swift movement he pulled her roughly into his arms and, as she gave a little cry of protest, his mouth came down on hers.

He kissed her brutally with lips that were hard and possessive. Though they hurt her, for the moment she was too surprised, too shocked, even to struggle.

Then, as she attempted it, she found that the Duke had imprisoned her arms to her sides and it was impossible to move or even to take her lips from him.

Her mouth was captive and she wanted not only to struggle against him but also to strike at him – to free herself as violently as he had taken her.

But she was unable to move.

Fiona had never been kissed by a man. She did not know how helpless a woman could be in a man's arms or when his mouth took possession of her.

His lips still hurt her and yet strangely the fury and the fear she had felt at first were now less intense.

Now the pain had gone and instead his lips were more gentle and yet still possessive.

'I must free myself! I must struggle!' Fiona thought feverishly.

Then, even as she tried to do so, she felt as if something strange that she had never known before was happening to her.

It was as if a warm wave inexplicably, indefinably rose through her body, passing through her breasts, up her throat and into her lips while they were still bruised from the intensity of the Duke's kiss.

It was such a strange and totally unexpected feeling that for a moment Fiona could think of nothing else, conscious that in some extraordinary manner it was intensifying, deepening, becoming more insistent.

She felt the Duke's arms tighten round her and yet instead of making her afraid she felt as if they gave her a security, something which swept away fear.

It was impossible to analyse and yet it was there, while the feeling in her throat grew into something wonderful, something incredibly like a rapture that seemed to encompass her and ripple through her like the waves of the sea.

It was an emotion she could not understand, but she was no longer fighting against the wonder of what she felt.

She savoured it, felt it envelop her until her mouth was soft beneath the Duke's and her body was no longer tense in his arms.

It was then that he raised his head. She was free and yet she could not move, could not speak, could not even think.

"God damn you!" he muttered hoarsely and his voice seemed to come from the very depths of his being.

Then, as violently as he had taken her, he left, walking quickly down the passage, his kilt swinging behind him.

Fiona almost fell and yet somehow she managed to reach out and hold on to a piece of furniture that stood against the wall.

For a long time she just stood there, trying to realise what had happened, trying to understand what she had felt, striving to think coherently –

Then slowly, so slowly that every footstep was an effort, she reached her room and threw herself face-downwards onto the bed.

*

In the morning light Fiona found it even harder to believe that what had happened was not just a figment of her imagination or some strange unaccountable dream.

Last night when she had finally taken off her dressing gown, she had crept into bed to lie sleepless, trying to understand not only that the Duke had kissed her in anger and what she supposed was jealousy, but also that it had aroused in her a rapture which even now did not seem credible.

Yet it had happened and no amount of introspection could alter the realisation that she had not been able to fight against the manner in which he had possessed her.

Instead she had acquiesced, finding an ecstasy that she had not expected, a rapture she had never imagined was possible.

'Perhaps I am mad?' Fiona questioned, but she knew that that was not the explanation.

It was difficult to rouse herself to give Mary-Rose her breakfast and to answer her chattering questions coherently.

"Yes, your uncle has said you may learn to fish."

"Yes, I will see if we can possibly do it this morning."

"Yes, it will be just the same way your father fished when he was your age."

"Yes!"

"Yes!"

"Yes!"

A dozen questions and, with the difficulty Fiona had in answering them, she might have been talking in an unfamiliar foreign language.

After they had visited Rollo in the kennels, which they did every morning and Mary-Rose had fed him a titbit from her breakfast, they settled down to some elementary lessons.

"I want to play the piano, Aunt Fiona."

"You must do your arithmetic first, dearest."

"Oh why? Sums are so boring. I know my tables."

It was a conversation that took place every morning and yet somehow this morning it seemed unfamiliar, just as everything else did.

Mr. McKeith sent a message to say that at eleven o'clock Donald would be waiting downstairs to take Mary-Rose to the river. There would be a pony for her to ride and one for Fiona.

Any other day, Fiona thought, she would have been excited at the thought of riding one of the shaggy little Scottish ponies which she knew carried the game out shooting and the stalkers when they had a long way to go before they started their stalk.

But this morning she felt as though her whole body was numb from the touch of the Duke's lips.

All she could feel were his arms imprisoning her and an echo of that strange yet wonderful sensation moving into her throat.

Because Donald was happy and content to listen to Mary-Rose's questions about her father, Fiona was free to think her own thoughts.

When they reached the river, he showed the child how to cast a line.

He was a willing teacher and, because Mary-Rose was ready to do exactly as he told her, she caught the knack of it very quickly.

"Look, Aunt Fiona, look at the lovely straight line I am throwing!" she was crying after a little while.

Then there was wild excitement when she caught a small salmon par.

It was a very tiny catch, but enough to send Mary-Rose into a fervour of excitement and keep her talking about it all the way home.

They entered The Castle and Fiona had no idea if the Duke was in the house or was lunching in the dining room.

Only when Mary-Rose had been put to bed for her rest, still talking about the fish she intended to catch tomorrow and Fiona had returned to the school room, did a servant open the door.

"His Grace wishes to see you in the library, miss!"

For a moment it was impossible to answer. Then in a voice that did not sound in the least like her own Fiona said,

"Please tell His Grace – I will be with him – in a few moments."

She would need a few moments, she thought, to compose herself, to think what she could say, to find words in which to explain that she had not been doing what he had suspected but had been on an errand of mercy.

Yet, why should she explain?

He had insulted her and she should force an apology from him. How dare he think she was the sort of woman who would behave in such a manner?

It was, of course, just what his father had suspected of Rosemary and it was obvious that she must expect the same treatment.

However, she was thankful that she had Jeannie to give evidence as to why he had found her out of her bedroom!

Mrs. Meredith had told her first thing this morning that Jeannie was better and, when Fiona went to see her, she found, as she had hoped, that the fever was broken.

"I will come and see her again this afternoon," Fiona had promised Mrs. Meredith.

"She looks better, miss, she does really," the house keeper replied. Those herbs of yourn must be wonderful – real magic, as her Ladyship'd say."

Fiona hesitated a moment.

"I hope if she says that she is joking, Mrs. Meredith. There is no magic in herbs, as you well know. Just common sense."

"I knows that, miss," Mrs. Meredith replied, "and don't you take any notice of her Ladyship's carryings on!"

Fiona looked at the housekeeper enquiringly as she added,

"You're too pretty for the task you've set yourself, miss and that's the truth. It's married you should be with a husband to fight your battles for you."

Fiona laughed.

"I hope I can fight my own battles, Mrs. Meredith."

"A man's awful handy at times," Mrs. Meredith retorted.

It suddenly struck Fiona that that was what she wanted now – a man to fight her battles for her. A man to explain to the Duke that she had not been behaving immorally as he had obviously suspected.

'How dare he?' she asked herself.

Fiona tried to hate him as she had done ever since she had arrived at The Castle, but somehow it was impossible.

She could never afterwards remember how she found her way down the long passage that led to the top of the stairs.

On one side of a wide landing there was the drawing room and on the other side to the left of the dining room was the library.

It was an extremely impressive room, lined from floor to ceiling with books, but, as Fiona walked into it, she had eyes only for the man waiting for her.

He was standing in front of the fireplace at the far end and she knew that she had a long way to walk towards him.

She felt her heart begin to beat violently in her breast and after one quick look she could only lower her eyes and her lashes were dark against her pale cheeks.

It was ridiculous, absurd, but she realised that she was trembling and somehow, without her willing them to do so, her feet were carrying her to him.

'I have to make him understand – I have to explain,' she kept thinking.

Then she was in front of him and, without even raising her eyes, she was vividly conscious of his presence.

'I must curtsey,' she thought, 'then I must begin to explain – '

But before she could move, before she could speak, the Duke said in a voice that she barely recognised,

"I want to apologise. You must forgive me."

Chapter Five

It seemed as if a very long time passed before Fiona could raise her eyes and look up at the Duke.

Then the expression she saw on his face made her draw in her breath.

"I have no excuse," he said, still in the low voice he had used before, "except that you drove me insane with jealousy and I thought in my madness that you had been with Torquil."

"How could you – think – such a – thing?" Fiona stammered.

She meant to sound angry, but her voice seemed only breathless.

"I told you that I was insane," the Duke replied.

As they stood looking at each other, Fiona thought that she was looking at a stranger and yet at the same time their minds were so attuned that there was no need for explanations, no need for apologies.

"Forgive me," the Duke repeated.

Then, before she could reply, he added,

"What are we to do about us? Tell me, for I have lain awake all night fighting against my anger. Now I know how despicably I behaved, but I still have found no solution to the problem."

Because she was bewildered and did not know what to say, Fiona felt that she must go back to the beginning and clear away what he had believed about her before they progressed any further.

"You know – now," she asked, "that I had been – trying to help – Jeannie?"

"Mrs. Meredith told me this morning how miraculously your herbs had worked. I then realised what a fool I had made of myself."

He looked into her eyes as he said,

"But I would not have it otherwise. When I kissed you, I found myself in Heaven after being in Hell for so long that I did not recognise that there was any other existence for me."

"I only learnt – yesterday of the – terrible suspicions that are – directed against– you," Fiona said hesitatingly.

"Torquil told you, I suppose," the Duke said sharply.

She thought his tone was critical and she answered,

"He thought I – ought to know because I – questioned him as to why – you were so – isolated here."

"And when he told you, what did you feel?"

She knew that there was a depth of feeling behind the question, which made her answer in all sincerity,

"I was – sorry, so very – sorry."

"I don't want your pity!"

"I am not offering you that. The Earl believes in you."

"And you?"

Fiona looked into his eyes and knew the truth.

"I know that you could not commit murder."

The Duke gave a sound that was a cry of triumph and put out his arms. Then, as if with a superhuman effort, he dropped them again.

"Do you really believe in me?" he asked.

Fiona nodded.

For the moment she could not trust herself to speak.

"Then nothing else matters," he said. "But you still have not answered my question. What can we do about *us*?"

Fiona made a helpless little gesture.

"What can we do?"

The Duke took a deep breath before he declared,

"You know if it was possible I would ask you to marry me."

Fiona felt as if the whole room was suddenly flooded with sunlight.

Then because the intensity of his voice left her with no words in which to reply, she merely looked at the Duke. Their eyes were held by each other's and she felt herself quiver.

It was as if he was kissing her again, as if he had evoked again that strange rapturous sensation she had felt the night before.

They were enchanted, held by a spell that enveloped them to the point where everything was forgotten except themselves and there were no horrifying suspicions and no longer a background of feuds and cruelty.

There was only a man and a woman who were caught up in something so primitive and yet so divine that nothing was of any consequence except that they belonged to each other.

"I knew the moment I saw you," the Duke said in a voice that shook.

"What – did you – know?"

"That I loved you!"

"How could you have – known that? I was – hating you."

"I was aware of what you felt and I understood why. I had hated myself far more bitterly than you ever could, since I had learnt of Ian's death."

Fiona looked at him in surprise and he carried on,

"I wanted to tell you, I wanted to explain ever since you came to The Castle. I suppose it was my pride that prevented me from doing so and in a way I wanted you to hate me."

Fiona looked perplexed and he smiled.

It illuminated his face, sweeping away the bitterness and the cynical lines that made him look older than his years.

"You hated me before you saw me," he said, "and I would have hated you if I had known of your existence."

"It was what I – expected."

"Then you walked into this room and I saw that you looked like an older replica of Mary-Rose, lovely like a shaft of sunlight against the darkness which has encompassed me for so long. I felt in that moment as if my whole world had turned topsy-turvy!"

"Can that be – true?"

"Come and sit down and I will tell you about it," the Duke suggested.

She had not moved from the spot where she had stopped to face him and now, feeling dazed, she looked round for somewhere to sit, then felt the Duke's hand on her arm, guiding her towards the sofa.

At the touch of him, she felt a streak like lightning flash through her. It made her draw in her breath and she sensed that he felt the same.

His eyes sought hers before he asked,

'How can we fight against that?"

Fiona sank down on the sofa, feeling, as she did so, as if her legs would no longer have supported her. The Duke sat beside her, turning his body to face her, his arm resting along the back of the sofa.

"I want to tell you about my behaviour to Ian," he began, "because I cannot bear to think that I should ever see again the hatred that was in your eyes the first time you looked at me."

"I thought you were – cruel and – unjust."

"I knew that and yet I believed there was nothing I could do."

"Explain it to me – please," Fiona asked.

"When Ian wrote to my father to say that he was to be married to a woman who had appeared in public and taken money for doing so, I suppose, if I am honest, I was almost as shocked as he was."

"It was because we needed – money to pay for my father's – illness."

"The idea of play-actresses being wicked was so deeply ingrained in my father's mind," the Duke said, "that it was impossible for him to differentiate between an actress and a musician. But *I* should have known better."

He paused before he continued,

"After the initial shock of Ian marrying anybody, especially a woman who was not Scottish, I think I should have written to him or, if I had been able, gone South to see him."

"You could not do that?" Fiona questioned.

"My father would have killed me if I had told him that that was what I intended to do and, when he learnt that Ian had actually married, he became so angry that if it had been possible I think he would have exercised the ancient Chieftain's right of life and death over his family and his followers and had him executed."

"It seems — extraordinary!" Fiona murmured. "But I suppose I can understand a – little of what he – felt."

"It would be impossible for you to do so," the Duke answered, "unless you had lived in the tightly knit community of a Scottish Clan like ours, who have kept aloof even from other Clans."

"But when your father died," Fiona asked, "could you not then have got in – touch with Ian?"

"That was, of course, what I had intended to do," the Duke said. "Ian and I had been so close and had meant so much to each other that I believed he would understand that as long as my father was alive it was impossible for me to defy the old man, even for someone I loved."

"But what – happened?" Fiona asked.

"I suppose members of a family are sometimes so closely attuned to each other that they are perceptive enough to read each other's thoughts. My father must have sensed what I intended to do."

There was a pause and after a moment Fiona asked again,

"What – happened?"

"On his death bed my father made me swear on the dirk, the most solemn and sacred vow any Scotsman can take, that I would not get in touch with Ian."

"Oh no!"

"I hesitated before I did as he asked," the Duke went on. "Then somehow, with a sense of his authority over me, which I had known all my life, I capitulated, partly because he was dying and partly because whatever his faults, I genuinely revered and admired him."

"It must have been difficult for you."

"I made one mental reservation," the Duke continued. "I felt obliged to keep my vow, but I told myself that if ever Ian tried to be in touch with me, that would not have been of my conniving and I could therefore respond to him."

Fiona clasped her hands together.

"If only he had known! He waited, longing to hear from you, finding it hard to believe that you would – ostracise him as his father had done."

"Should I have broken my vow?"

The question was sudden, and Fiona knew by the way the Duke spoke that her answer was very important to him.

For a moment she did not reply. She knew he was tense, waiting to hear her condemn him as she had done for so long, not knowing the facts.

Then she said quietly,

"Knowing how much the ideals and the traditions of the Clan mean to a man like you, I don't think it possible for you to have broken a vow made in such circumstances."

She saw the relief in the Duke's eyes before he cried,

"It is what I expected you to reply. Oh, my darling, how can you be everything that I admire and revere in life, not only your beauty but your character and your understanding!"

Fiona put up her hands in a little gesture as if to protect herself from him.

"You must – not say such – things. We were talking of Ian. I only wish that he could have understood the – situation. It would have made him very much – happier."

"If he had known, he *would* have understood," the Duke said. "Our father was to both of us not only a paternal figure, he was also our Chieftain. We did whatever he asked of us, believing that to disobey was an act of treachery."

Fiona smiled.

"And yet Ian, knowing that, married my sister because he loved her."

"That was something I never understood until now, but you have shown me that love is stronger than the allegiance of blood, stronger than a thousand years of tradition."

Fiona looked away from him.

"I am not sure you should say that," she said. "I am beginning to understand how important your position is. To me it is another world, but it is one in which you reign supreme."

"Not supreme," the Duke said. "I doubt if the Clan trusts me as they trusted my father."

"How can – anyone think you – guilty of such a crime?" Fiona asked.

"The Rannocks would fight and die for me," the Duke said simply. "They would follow me wherever I chose to lead them. But I know that many of those around me question whether my wife's disappearance was not of my contriving."

"I think that is only your opinion."

"I naturally could not speak of such things to anyone else!"

"I have seen the expression," Fiona said, "in the eyes of the men and women in The Castle and I think that they, like the Earl, know you are incapable – of doing anything dishonourable or wicked."

As if he could not help himself, the Duke reached out and took her hand and raised it to his lips.

"Thank you," he sighed. "I told you that you are a shaft of sunlight and now you have given me a light in my heart that has not been there for many years."

Fiona felt herself tremble not only at what he said but because his lips had touched her hand.

She knew that she wanted, with an intensity that frightened her, for him to kiss her as he had kissed her the night before.

Once again, as if he knew what she was thinking, he raised his eyes to look at her and say,

"That is what I want too and, because we both feel like this, my precious one, I shall have to send you away."

It was something she had not expected him to say and Fiona gave a little cry.

"No, no! You cannot do – that!"

"Do you think I can let you stay?" he asked. "You know already how uncontrollable I can be."

"At least I should – see you," Fiona whispered.

"Would that be enough for either of us?" he asked, "I want you! I want you as my wife. I want you in my arms now at this moment and every night for the rest of my life. Do you really believe, loving you as I do, that I could keep my distance?"

As he spoke, he relinquished her hand and rose from the sofa.

As if he could not bear to look at her, he walked towards the window to stand staring out with unseeing eyes.

Fiona did not move, she only clasped her hands together and, as she did so, she could still feel the pressure of his lips on her skin.

"I cannot – go!" she whispered. "I cannot – leave you."

"You have to, my sweet. Give me a few days and I will make the excuse that Mary-Rose needs a fuller education than we can give her here. Then you can go to Edinburgh. I have a house there which can be opened for you and you will find plenty of people glad to entertain you."

Even as he spoke, he brought his clenched fist down sharply on the windowsill.

"And there will be men!" he exclaimed. "Men who will be blinded by your beauty as I have been! God, how can I think of it?"

There was so much pain beneath the words that Fiona rose from the sofa and moved to stand beside him.

"Everything is – moving too – fast," she said. "Please don't make – plans yet. Let us have time to think."

"What is there to think about?" he asked harshly.

"That we love each other."

"I have told you that that is something I dare not consider – not unless you wish me to behave like the barbarian you thought me to be when you came North."

"I did not think that," Fiona contradicted him, "and I don't think that you would behave like one now."

She spoke softly and he turned to look at her, standing with her eyes raised to his, the light from the window revealing the clarity of her skin and the softness of her parted lips.

"If you look at me like that," he said hoarsely, "I swear, if I was married to a thousand women, I would still take you and make you mine as you were intended to be."

The passion in his voice seemed to vibrate between them, but Fiona was not afraid. Instead she put out her hand and laid it on his arm.

"I love you," she said simply. "And we will – fight this – together. Somehow, with God's help, we will find the – proof that your wife is – dead."

"Proof?" the Duke echoed. "Do you not think I have searched for it? I have questioned everybody and I had the whole countryside combed for any trace of her. But there has been nothing to give us any clue as to what happened."

"But there must be something. No one can disappear completely, no one can die without leaving their body behind."

"Do you suppose I have not thought of that? I have had the river dragged and I have had the foresters walk over every inch of the ground within miles of The Castle."

"And *inside*?" Fiona asked.

"We have been through the dungeons and we have searched every Tower and examined almost every stone, without finding even a footprint."

"And yet, if she is alive, she must be somewhere," Fiona said quietly. "And if she is dead, then there will be her bones, if nothing else."

"Then let's find her!"

"That is what I want to help you to do," Fiona answered. "Even if I was not personally interested, I would not think it right for you, a young man, to be tied for the rest of your life to a woman who is quite obviously dead."

"You are personally interested?" the Duke asked.

'Do you want me to – tell you how – much?"

"You know that is what I am asking. Tell me, my darling, because, although I can see it in your eyes and hear it in the tone of your voice, I also want to listen to the words themselves."

He waited.

Then Fiona said, the colour rising in her cheeks,

"You are – making me – shy."

"It makes you even more beautiful than you are already."

He took her hand in his and, turning it over, pressed his lips to the palm, and as he did so, he felt the quiver that swept through Fiona.

"Now tell me," he asked softly.

"I – love – you!" she whispered and her fingers closed over his.

"That is what I want you to say and, because you have said it, I swear I will fight again to be free so that I can make you mine."

He bent his head and, opening her hand, kissed her palm again.

Then his lips were on her wrist and she felt a strange feeling seep like lightning through her that was half-pain, half-pleasure.

"Oh, my precious, my sweet!" the Duke sighed. "I can make you feel a little of what I am feeling, but there is more, so much more that I could teach you!"

With an effort Fiona took her hand from his.

"We must be – sensible," she said breathlessly. "We have to go into – battle – that is what it must be, a battle – using our brains."

The Duke's eyes were on her lips as she spoke.

Then he said,

"I want to kiss you. God knows it is the hardest thing I have ever done not to do so, not to know again the ecstasy I felt last night, even though I was so angry."

"It was – wonderful for – me too," Fiona whispered, "but I have a feeling that we have to earn that – wonder before we can – enjoy it."

"Suppose – suppose we fail to find what we are seeking, as I have failed in the past years?"

Fiona smiled.

"Mary-Rose has called me a White Witch and Lady Morag paints me a different colour. But whatever I may be, I have the feeling – the unmistakable conviction – that if we fight – together, you and I, we shall win!"

"I want to believe you, Fiona, I want it with all my heart and soul! At the same time, my precious, I can see the difficulties and I will not have you talked about."

"Who is likely to do so?" Fiona asked lightly.

As she spoke she remembered Lady Morag.

"Exactly!" the Duke said as if she had spoken aloud. "She is a very tiresome possessive woman. I don't think you can be friends with her."

"I have no wish to be," Fiona replied, "and it has annoyed me the way she has talked about witchcraft, although I think that most of the servants are too sensible to listen to her."

"One never knows," the Duke said, "but the physician, I understand, has returned by now and in the future he will be sent for in the usual way."

Fiona gave a little cry.

"Surely that is capitulation? It is a superstition which is not only ridiculous but has no basis in truth."

"The Scots are superstitious and Lady Morag can by her foolish words inflame old prejudices."

"What you are really saying," Fiona said with a smile, "is that because I am a Sassenach I might easily be a *black* witch!"

The Duke laughed.

"I don't imagine that anyone in their senses could believe that you can cast spells or fly to a Sabbath on your broomstick. Equally it is easy to inflame people against such things when they live in such confined circumstances and have little to talk about outside their own lives."

~131~

Fiona was silent for a moment.

Then she said,

"Are you really telling me not to help people like Jeannie when I know my herbs can take away their fever or cure an infected hand?"

"I think perhaps at the moment it would be wise not to do any more than you have done already."

"It seems ridiculous!"

"I know," he agreed, "but if you are to stay here, my darling, we must be careful that there are no poisonous tongues saying things that might eventually harm you. That I could never bear!"

He gave a deep sigh.

"Perhaps I am wrong. You have persuaded me to let you stay, but I have a feeling which I cannot quite explain, that you would be safer, and not only from me, in Edinburgh."

"If you want me here," Fiona said, "I would not be such a coward as to run away."

"Want you?" the Duke repeated. "Have you any idea how much I want you or how difficult it is going to be to live without you?"

He looked away from her as he said,

"If you were wise, you would accept Torquil and leave me to my ghosts."

"If you are suggesting that the Earl has proposed marriage to me, he has done nothing of the sort."

"But he will ask you," the Duke replied positively. "I have seen the way he looks at you! I have heard the note

~132~

in his voice when he talks about you when we are alone, which has never been there before. He is already in love with you."

He paused before he added,

"That is why last night when I thought you had been to his room I behaved in such a manner that I am really surprised you could deign to speak to me again!"

He looked at her as he finished speaking and, as their eyes met, there was no need for Fiona to answer him.

They just looked at each other for what seemed a long time.

Then the Duke said,

"God knows I am afraid of losing you. Oh, my darling, I feel as if I was a prisoner incarcerated in a dungeon and suddenly for the first time there is a light that I have never seen before."

Without being conscious of what she was doing, Fiona took a step towards him, then without either of them consciously realising what was happening the Duke's arms were round her and she was close against him.

His lips came down on hers.

It was then she knew that the rapture and ecstasy she had felt last night were but a pale reflection of the wonder he evoked in her now, when they had both of them acknowledged their love.

His lips seemed to draw her very heart and soul from her body and make them his and she felt as if her whole being vibrated to the music that came from him and yet was part of a celestial choir.

There was sunshine and a melody of such wonder that it ran through their hearts and minds and through every nerve of their bodies until they were no longer two people but one, held together by a power that came from outside themselves and filled them with all the vibrations of the Universe.

'I love you! I love you!' Fiona wanted to shout out.

But the Duke held her lips and she could only feel as if their love was part of their very breath and as necessary to them both as life itself.

'I could never leave him,' she told herself and knew, without his saying so, that he would never let her go.

His love swept her up into the sky and she felt as though they flew into the very heart of the sun and were burning in the fire of it.

Then when the wonder and the miracle of it were almost too much to endure, Fiona gave a little murmur and hid her face against the Duke's shoulder.

She quivered with the emotions he had evoked in her and she felt his lips on her hair.

"I love you!" he said in a voice deep and unsteady. "I adore you, my darling, and there is nothing else in the whole world except you."

"It does not seem – possible that I can – feel like – this," Fiona mumbled.

The Duke's arms tightened round her and as they did so the clock on the mantelpiece chimed the hour.

Fiona gave a start.

"Mary-Rose!" she exclaimed. "I had forgotten about her! I must go to her. It is time for her to get up from her rest."

"I think we have both forgotten everything but ourselves," the Duke said. "Somehow I will arrange that we shall sometimes be together and alone, but you will understand, my precious, that it will not be easy. I have no wish for the servants to be aware of our feelings for each other."

Fiona smiled at him.

"We will be very circumspect," she said, "but I shall be thinking of you."

"I think it would be impossible for either of us to think of anything else," the Duke replied, "and do not forget for one instant that I love you."

"As I love you," Fiona answered.

It was like a physical pain to move away from his arms.

Then, because she felt that if she looked at him again she would be unable to leave the room, she walked very quickly to the door, opened it and went out onto the landing.

She could see the kilted figures of two footmen below in the hall and she wondered if they had noticed her go into the library and were thinking it strange that she had been there for so long.

Then because she knew that Mary-Rose would be waiting for her she ran down the passage to the child's bedroom.

*

It was with excitement mixed with apprehension that Fiona went to the drawing room before dinner that evening.

Excitement because she would see the Duke again and had found, as he had anticipated, that it was impossible to think of anything else but him all the afternoon.

And apprehension because she was aware that Lady Morag would be dining that evening as she always dined on Wednesday nights, also because she was afraid that the Earl might sense that something unexpected had happened.

She knew that the Duke and the Earl had gone fishing late in the afternoon when Mary-Rose had wanted to see Rollo and found the kennel empty.

"His Grace has taken him with him, miss," Angus had told the child, adding, "He's gone to catch a big fish for your dinner if he be lucky."

"I would like to have gone with him," Mary-Rose replied and Fiona echoed the same words in her own heart.

They explored parts of The Castle grounds that they had not seen before and talked with various members of the staff who all wanted to meet Mary-Rose.

"She's a bonnie wee lassie," one of the older men said to Fiona. "I can see the likeness to his Lordship in her, sure enough."

Fiona thought this was wishful thinking since Mary-Rose was in fact a replica of her mother and had none of her father's characteristics.

She thought to herself that people saw what they expected to see and she wondered if that might be a clue as to where the Duchess might be hidden.

Perhaps everything she had done on that particular day when she disappeared had been so ordinary that nobody had noticed it and yet it might have had some significance.

When they returned to The Castle they met Mr. McKeith in the passage and Mary-Rose, who was very fond of him, slipped her hand into his.

"You promised to show me the room where you work, Mr. McKeith," she said.

"So I did," he replied. "Well, come and see it now and you'll see how busy I am."

He took her into a large and rather impressive office on the ground floor, where besides a large desk piled with papers there were boxes bearing the Ducal crown and large maps of the estate.

Mary-Rose danced round looking at everything and Fiona said to Mr. McKeith,

"Why did you not tell me when we were talking about the Duchess's disappearance that the Duke was under suspicion?"

Mr. McKeith looked startled at her question.

"I did not think it necessary," he said after a moment.

"I thought it strange that there were so few visitors."

"It's a very sad state of affairs," Mr. McKeith agreed.

"Not only sad for His Grace but also for Mary-Rose. She cannot grow up without friends of her own age. In fact I hoped there would be children to share some of her lessons with her."

"I daresay there are children of the same age about," Mr. McKeith said doubtfully.

"You know exactly what I mean," Fiona said. "I am told there are many important families near here and some of them must have children who would be the right sort of friends for Mary-Rose."

Mr. McKeith looked uncomfortable.

Then he said,

"I will see what I can do about it, Miss Windham."

"There is only one thing any of us can do," Fiona replied, "and that is to prove how the Duchess died."

If she had intended to startle Mr. McKeith, she certainly succeeded.

"I told you that every effort has been made," he replied after a moment, "but unsuccessfully. I don't know what else we can do."

"Sometimes a stranger coming new to a problem can find a solution where others have failed," Fiona remarked.

"What are you suggesting?" Mr. McKeith enquired.

"There must be a report made by the Sheriff at the time. I would like to see it."

"I don't know whether His Grace – " Mr. McKeith began.

"I think it would be embarrassing for me to have to ask His Grace for it," Fiona interrupted. "That is why, Mr. McKeith, I am asking you."

He seemed to hesitate for a moment.

Then as if he made up his mind he said,

"Very well, Miss Windham. There are quite a number of papers concerning the Duchess's disappearance. I will collect them together and put them in a folder for you to study."

"Thank you," Fiona said with a smile, "and when I have read them, if there are any questions I would like to ask, I hope you will be kind enough to answer them."

"You intend to concern yourself with this problem, Miss Windham?"

"Anything that concerns my niece concerns me," Fiona replied firmly, "and there is no need for me to tell you, Mr. McKeith, that the state of affairs that exists now, if it continues, will undoubtedly affect Mary-Rose in the future."

She felt as if Mr. McKeith had suddenly succumbed to her insistence.

"I see your point, Miss Windham and it is something that did not strike me previously, but I am sure you are right."

"Then help me, please help me," Fiona begged.

"Of course. I will do anything in my power and I promise you that every report, every paper, every subsequent review of the situation will be in your hands within the next hour or so."

Fiona gave him a dazzling smile.

"Thank you, Mr. McKeith. And now I must give Mary-Rose her tea. Would you like to join us?"

"I should be very honoured to do so," Mr. McKeith replied, "and I hope you will ask me another day. But now I not only have a number of instructions from His Grace to be carried out but also yours."

"Then we will certainly ask you another time," Fiona smiled.

She called Mary-Rose and they went up the stairs hand in hand.

"This is a very big castle, Aunt Fiona," Mary-Rose said, "and not a bit like being at home, but I think I am going to be happy here."

"I am sure you are, dearest Mary-Rose," Fiona answered.

In her heart she sent up a prayer that this might in fact be true.

She was thinking of Mary-Rose's optimism when she entered the drawing room to see Lady Morag standing at the end of it, talking possessively in her usual manner to the Duke.

She was wearing a much smarter gown than she had worn on other occasions, and Fiona had the idea that she was deliberately attempting to outshine the Duke's English guest.

There were diamonds glittering in her ears and round her throat. There was also a glitter in her eyes that told Fiona only too clearly of her enmity.

"Good evening, Miss Windham!" she said as Fiona curtseyed to her. "And how is dear little Mary-Rose? I hope she is getting on with her lessons. I see from the windows of my house that you spend a great deal of time out of doors."

"Mary-Rose does some lessons in the schoolroom," Fiona replied, "but she is also learning while we are out of doors and, because she is an intelligent child, our conversation is often on quite advanced subjects."

"How lucky she is to have someone as clever as yourself to teach her," Lady Morag said.

It was obvious that she was being sarcastic from the way she looked Fiona up and down as she spoke, as if she was thinking that anybody who was pretty and smartly dressed was unlikely to have any brains in their head.

Fiona moved towards the Duke and murmured,

"Good evening, Your Grace."

It was only by the greatest effort of will that she prevented herself from looking at him as she spoke.

She knew if she once met his eyes it would be diffi-cult to look away and she was afraid too that Lady Morag would see the expression of love that she would be unable to suppress.

"Good evening, Miss Windham," the Duke replied gravely.

She told herself that she could hear his love vibrating beneath the simple commonplace words and that he was feeling as she was.

It was a relief to be able to turn to the Earl and ask animated questions about their fishing expedition.

"I was more successful this afternoon," he said. "In fact I have beaten the Duke by catching two salmon to his one."

"That is splendid and I must remember to tell Mary-Rose," Fiona replied.

Then they chattered on about what Angus had said when they went to visit Rollo.

"I am sure you ought not to go near that dog," the Earl said in a concerned manner, "Supposing he savages you? I don't think I could bear it!"

"I am sure Mary-Rose will protect me," Fiona said lightly.

She knew by the expression in the Earl's eyes that the Duke had been right when he said that he admired her.

She continued talking to the Earl, although she knew that she was encouraging him almost cruelly in his feelings towards her. But she dared not talk to the Duke for fear that they would betray themselves to Lady Morag.

Even so, she was certain that the Scottish woman was slightly suspicious, for after dinner when they withdrew into the drawing room, she said,

"It is difficult for me to bring up the subject again, Miss Windham, but I cannot help feeling that you must find life here very dull and it would be wise to consider returning to the South as soon as possible!"

"I have very few ties in the South," Fiona answered. "I lived with my sister and brother-in-law and so my home was theirs. Now all I have left is Mary-Rose."

"I can understand you loving the child," Lady Morag said, "but of course her position here will alter very considerably if the Duke should marry again."

"I understood that that is impossible – for the moment at any rate," Fiona replied.

"There is always the chance that the Duchess's body will be discovered," Lady Morag said, "in which case he will be free."

There was something in the way she spoke that made Fiona glance at her sharply.

Then insidiously the idea came to her that Lady Morag had a clue to the Duchess's whereabouts.

"As you live here, Lady Morag," she said aloud, "then surely you have some idea about what happened to His Grace's wife. It seems so extraordinary that she could disappear without a trace."

"Very extraordinary!" Lady Morag agreed. "But, of course, they were very unhappy together."

Again it seemed to Fiona that there was an undercurrent beneath Lady Morag's words, as if she hinted that in the circumstances the Duke was glad to be rid of her.

"The Earl told me that some people believe that the Duke was responsible for the Duchess's disappearance," Fiona ventured, "but knowing the character of my brother-in-law, I cannot believe that any relative of his could commit such a horrifying crime."

"Perhaps you have not had much experience of men and women when they are emotionally roused," Lady Morag said significantly.

Fiona's eyes widened.

"Are you suggesting, Lady Morag, that the Duke *is* guilty?"

She thought, as she spoke, that at least she was pushing the older woman into the open, forcing her to express her opinion of the situation.

Lady Morag gave an affected laugh.

"Really, Miss Windham! What an extraordinary question! Of course I would not think anything derogatory of the dear Duke! At the same time, if such ideas frighten you, perhaps you would be wise not to stay here unprotected."

Fiona laughed and it was a more genuine sound than Lady Morag's laughter.

"Now you are being dramatic, Lady Morag," she said. "I assure you I am not afraid that anyone would want to murder me! At the same time I hope for Mary-Rose's sake that the Duke is free to marry again. I don't think a woman, however exceptional, is really capable of being a good Chieftain."

She saw an expression in Lady Morag's eyes that told her, although it seemed too fantastic to be credible, that her suspicions were right.

Lady Morag could, she was sure, reveal the whereabouts of her sister or at least give a clue to them if she was certain that the Duke, once free, would marry her.

'Perhaps I am being ultra-perceptive or perhaps, because I mind so tremendously, I am imagining things,' Fiona thought to herself.

Later that night when she was in bed she went over the conversations she had had with Lady Morag, recalling every inflection of her voice and the expressions on her face.

She was now certain, quite certain, that Lady Morag knew a great deal more than she had told anybody and that she was also determined by every means in her power to capture the Duke.

'That is one thing she will never do.' Fiona thought. 'I will not only fight to set him free, but I will fight for him. I love him! He is mine! *Mine for all eternity*!'

Chapter Six

Mrs. Meredith helped Fiona off with her evening gown.

"You looked real pretty this evening, miss," she said. "They all commented on it downstairs."

"Thank you," Fiona replied and smiled.

Then, as Mrs. Meredith carried the gown towards the wardrobe, she asked,

"Was Lady Morag fond of her sister the Duchess?"

Mrs. Meredith stopped and turned round to look at Fiona as if she was surprised at the question.

Then she answered,

"She were indeed, miss. They were inseparable, you might say, which was why after her Ladyship's husband died the old Duke offered her a house in the grounds."

Fiona could not think of Lady Morag being devoted to a younger sister.

There was something hard and inflexible about her, except where her feelings towards the Duke were concerned.

"If you ask me," Mrs. Meredith went on, as if following the train of her own thoughts, "Lady Morag and Her Grace were too close. I used to feel somehow they were makin' His Grace the odd man out. But there, as my old mother used to say, 'two's company, three's none'!"

She took Fiona's gown to the wardrobe and when she had done so, Fiona said,

"Have you any ideas, Mrs. Meredith, as to what happened to the Duchess? Someone must have seen her the day she disappeared."

"I saw her, miss, and waited on Her Grace, as I always did."

"Did she seem quite normal – not upset or anything?"

"Not in the least, miss. Chattering away, she was, about a ball that was to be given here the followin' week."

"A ball," Fiona murmured as if to herself.

She was thinking how The Castle seemed made for such festivities and to entertain a large number of people.

Mr. McKeith had shown Mary-Rose and her the ballroom, which he said was originally called the 'Chief's Room' because it was where the Chief of the Clan gathered his Clansmen when they planned their offensives either against the English or against other Clans they were at war with.

The late Duke had renovated it as he had the other parts of The Castle and it now had a beauty and a grandeur that Fiona was sure made it very different from the way it had been in the days when it had been a closely fortified room with doubtless only arrow-slits to let in the light.

"Her Grace was very undecided as to which of her beautiful gowns she would wear," Mrs. Meredith was continuing. "At first she thought she'd wear white, so that the Rannock diamonds would sparkle on her dark hair, but Lady Morag felt that she should wear green. 'Green!'

she objected in my presence. 'But I think it's unlucky. Whenever I wear that colour I seem to have a row with Aiden'. 'Green will suit you best,' Lady Morag said firmly, 'and the emeralds will look magnificent with it'."

"I thought Lady Morag was very superstitious," Fiona murmured, remembering the fuss she had made about witchcraft.

Mrs. Meredith shrugged her shoulders.

"Her Ladyship says one thing one moment and another the next. But there, Her Grace never had a chance to prove whether green was unlucky or no."

When Mrs. Meredith left her, Fiona sat thinking.

Was there any significance to be found in the fact that Lady Morag, while loving her sister, had apparently not minded when she quarrelled with her husband?

It was perhaps in character with her obvious possessiveness and yet Fiona could not help thinking that there was something deeper behind the information she had received from Mrs. Meredith.

'Whatever I do,' she told herself, 'I must not let the servants think I am spying or being over-inquisitive, but their point of view is interesting and I doubt if anyone in The Castle has asked them what they felt about the Duchess's disappearance.'

She could not imagine the Duke discussing such personal matters with his valet and she was quite certain that Mr. McKeith, in his position, would think it beneath his dignity to gossip with the staff.

'I must find out all I can,' Fiona told herself, 'but I must be very very discreet about it.'

As she climbed into bed, she was thinking how wonderful it would be if she could discuss with the Duke everything she heard and everything she thought.

But she knew he had been right when he said that they must be very careful and she was sure that even the walls in The Castle had eyes as well as ears.

'But I want to see him,' she told herself and felt an irrepressible need for him.

It was not only that she yearned for the security of his arms and the touch of his lips. She knew already in so short a time that her love was much deeper than that.

There was an affinity between them that made her feel when they were together that they were complete – one person instead of two, joined by their minds, their instincts and the very beat of their hearts, until it seemed to Fiona as if she had no life of her own apart from him.

"I love – you!" she whispered into her pillow and wondered how they could go through life separated by a dead woman.

*

Mary-Rose was resting after luncheon and Fiona was playing very softly on the piano in the schoolroom when the door opened and the Earl came in.

"I was looking for you," he began. "I heard your music and it guided me here."

Fiona took her hands from the piano keys and laughed.

"You are becoming very poetical, my Lord."

"You know the reason," the Earl replied.

Fiona rose.

"Where is the Duke?" she asked to change the subject.

"He has a crowd of old men, wrapped up like bundles in their tartans, who have come down from the North to consult him on some knotty problem they cannot solve for themselves."

"I think the Clansmen's faith in their chief is very touching," Fiona remarked, as if she challenged the somewhat disparaging note in the Earl's voice.

"It is extraordinary how soft your heart is for people like that and how hard where I am concerned," he replied.

"As you are here, let's talk about something interesting," Fiona suggested.

"I can imagine nothing more interesting than you."

Fiona threw out her hands with a little gesture of helplessness.

"Please, you are making things very difficult for me."

The Earl looked at her and then said quietly,

"I suppose I had better face the fact that you are in love with Aiden."

Fiona looked at him wide-eyed and felt the blood sweep up her face.

"What do you – mean?"

"Exactly what I say and don't bother to deny it. I have seen you together."

Fiona clasped her hands.

"What – am I to – say?" she asked.

"Nothing," the Earl replied. "I suppose it was inevitable that such a thing should happen and because I love you both I might even be glad that Aiden has found happiness at last, if it was not such a hopeless situation."

"I like you for saying – that," Fiona said in a low voice.

"I want a great deal more from you than liking and because I love you, I cannot bear to see you break your heart over Aiden as you are bound to do."

"I thought that you might – help him to be – free."

"Help him?" the Earl questioned. "I have done everything I can."

"There must be something you have missed," Fiona insisted. "Something so obvious that nobody has thought of it."

"Heaven alone knows what it can be."

There was silence for a moment and then he said,

"The best course you can take, if you are sensible, is to marry me and forget Aiden and all the misery that exists here in his castle."

"Even if I wanted to marry you," Fiona answered, "you know that I could not leave Mary-Rose."

"I am perfectly prepared to look after her."

"Do you think the Rannocks would allow that? It would start up another Clan war."

The Earl sighed.

"Why could I not have met you in the ordinary way in the South and fallen in love with you? I could have persuaded you to marry me before you even set eyes on Aiden."

Fiona did not answer and after a moment he went on,

"I know what you are thinking and if you had never seen him I believe I could have made you love me. Where women are concerned they are always bowled over by his looks, his prestige and, of course, his indifference to them. No woman can resist that!"

He spoke bitterly and Fiona gave a little cry.

"Please – please," she pleaded. "I could not bear to spoil your friendship with the Duke, which, as you well know, is the – only thing he has – left."

She moved across the room to stand beside the Earl. She put her hand on his arm and said,

"I admire and respect you for the way you have been so loyal to your friend and, whatever – happens in the – future, he must never – lose you."

As if she appealed to something within him that the Earl found slightly embarrassing, he looked away from her.

Then he said,

"You are making me into a hero and I like it!"

Fiona gave a little laugh and took her hand from his arm.

"Then be a Scottish hero and fight this monstrous mystery. The Scots always enjoy a battle."

"What do you know about them?" the Earl queried.

"Only that since I have been in Scotland I have met two of the finest men that could exist anywhere in the world."

"Thank you, even though I come number two on the list," the Earl said. "And now, about this mystery – how do you suggest we start solving it when the best detectives available have failed?"

"I wish I knew the answer," Fiona replied. "But I have been reading the Sheriffs' and the Police reports and it seems to me that everyone was quite certain that the Duchess left The Castle."

"The inside of every part of it was searched thoroughly."

"I wonder," Fiona said. "I cannot help feeling that there was something that was overlooked and I believe the person who could help us, if she wished to do so, is Lady Morag."

She obviously startled the Earl, who stared at her in astonishment.

"Lady Morag?" he repeated. "If she knows anything I should be surprised."

"Why do you say that?"

"Because she made such a fuss when it first happened, weeping, wailing, fainting and begging everybody to search the forest, the river, the moors and even insisting on going with some of the search parties of foresters and Clansmen."

"Do you believe her grief was genuine?" Fiona asked quietly.

"She certainly made a tremendous demonstration of it and, of course, she clung to Aiden, making their joint loss an excuse to be constantly with him."

Fiona looked at him sharply.

"She was in love with the Duke even then?"

"I suppose so," the Earl replied. "I must say I did not take much notice of her before the Duchess's death. I have always found her a very unattractive woman."

"Think back," Fiona suggested. "Try to remember if she appeared to want to be with the Duke as much as she wanted to be with her sister."

There was silence for a minute.

"I am trying to recall what happened when they were together," the Earl said after a little while. "I know I used to think it must be a nuisance for Aiden to have his sister-in-law always with them. Then I thought perhaps it was a relief as he did not get on with his wife."

"Was that obvious?"

"It was obvious to me," the Earl replied. "Of course, having been such a close friend of Aiden's for so long, I knew that at first he did not wish to marry Janet and then, when he did, they quarrelled continually – "

"Why did they?" Fiona asked.

"I told you that I did not think she was entirely normal and Lady Morag admitted to me once that she used to have such uncontrollable tantrums when she was a child that they had to give her special medicines to calm her down."

"In which case," Fiona said, "do you think that when she was in a rage or a tantrum or whatever you like to call it, she did away with herself?"

"It's a possibility," the Earl admitted.

"And if she did – how?"

"Aiden had every river and every loch within walking distance of The Castle dredged."

"It seems extraordinary, but somehow we have to find an explanation."

She looked at the Earl as she spoke and, after a moment, he said,

"I know what you are asking me. I will help you, but I must say I think it is extremely generous of me in the circumstances."

"I think it is very wonderful of you," Fiona replied quietly. "But I would not expect you to do anything different."

"That's not fair!" he protested. "What I want to do, as you well know, is to pick you up in my arms, carry you away and make you forget Aiden and his disappearing wife and the gloom of The Castle, which becomes more like a tomb every time I visit it."

"As it is, because you are *you*," Fiona said, "you will help me and the Duke to find happiness."

For a moment the Earl did not speak, then he gave a deep sigh before he admitted,

"All right! You win! It is just my accursed luck to play the supporting role instead of the lead!"

"Thank you," Fiona said simply.

Then she looked at the clock.

"It is time for me to waken Mary-Rose after her rest."

"Which I suppose is a gentle hint that I can get myself lost," the Earl sighed. "What are you going to do?"

"We are going fishing."

"Can I come with you?"

"I would like you to, but I think it would be a mistake. I am quite sure that, when the Duke has finished with the Clansmen, he will want you with him."

"If you go on at me like this," the Earl threatened, "I shall return to my own castle and the gaieties that are waiting for me there!"

Fiona knew that it was an idle threat and she merely smiled at him.

"You are needed here," she said, "and so I feel in my bones that you will stay."

She saw the rueful expression on the Earl's face as she left the room.

*

That evening the three of them were alone at dinner and, because the Earl set himself out to be amusing and make the Duke laugh, it was the gayest meal Fiona had enjoyed since she had come to The Castle.

The Earl told stories of various escapades when they were boys and, as she watched the Duke laughing, she thought how different everything would be if he was not oppressed by the shadow a woman had cast over him and his life.

'If anything can be a witch's spell, it is that menacing evil, like a fog, from which it is impossible for him to escape,' she told herself.

They were still joking after dinner was finished and the two men joined Fiona in the drawing room.

"Shall I be tactful and leave you two alone?" the Earl enquired.

Before Fiona could speak, the Duke said,

"No. It would be a mistake."

They both looked at him in surprise at his positiveness and he explained,

"I learnt only today that the third footman who was engaged about two months ago is the son of Morag's cook and I have a feeling that anything that is said or done will be repeated in Battlement House."

"I am quite certain it will be!" the Earl remarked. "How did you learn this?"

"Morag said something to me the other evening," the Duke answered, "which I knew I had discussed only with you at breakfast and had in fact not mentioned it to anyone else, not even McKeith. It did not strike me at the time as being peculiar."

He paused before he continued,

"But today, as I was thinking how important it was that there should be no gossip attached to Fiona, I asked Mr. McKeith about the new servants in The Castle and he told me that Morag had asked him particularly to engage her cook's son."

"An unfortunate situation," the Earl remarked, "for you can hardly sack him."

"No, of course not," the Duke agreed, "but it means that we shall have to be particularly careful. For you to leave Fiona and me alone at this moment would therefore be a mistake."

"I can see that," Fiona said, "and actually I think it would be best for me to retire to bed. I have a feeling that, although she thinks of me as a Governess, Lady Morag also feels that I should be chaperoned."

"I have thought that too," the Duke said, "and it is something I intend to discuss with you when we have the opportunity."

"Have you no relative, preferably old and rather blind, who could come and stay for a little while?" Fiona suggested.

"I shall have to think about it," the Duke said with a smile. "I cannot remember one offhand."

He spoke lightly, but his eyes met Fiona's as he did so and she knew that he was saying to her without words that what he wanted more than anything in the world was for them to be alone.

He made no movement, but she felt as if he was reaching out towards her and she knew that it was only by an effort of willpower that she stopped her feet from carrying her swiftly into his arms.

For a moment she had forgotten the Earl and even where they were.

She just felt as if the room vanished and she had only to lift her lips to the Duke for him to hold her captive.

Her love welled up inside her almost like a tidal wave and she knew that the Duke felt the same and that even though they were not touching each other they were close spiritually, mentally and physically in a way that was impossible to define.

'*I love you*!' Fiona felt the words tremble on her lips.

Then she forced herself to curtsey to smile at the Earl, and to begin to walk across the room.

Before she could reach the door, the Duke was there and they both put out their hands towards the handle at the same moment.

As their fingers touched, Fiona felt not only a streak of lightning sweep through her, as it always did when she touched him, but she sensed that the same feeling brought him an agony that she could see in his eyes and a sudden tightening of his lips.

She knew that the control he imposed on himself was strained until one day it would reach the breaking point.

'I must be careful,' she thought.

Then, when she reached her bedroom, she thought that perhaps she should go away.

'How can we go on forever as we are?' she asked herself.

She wondered if it would be kinder to the Duke and more sensible to accept his first suggestion to move to Edinburgh with Mary-Rose.

Everything in her body cried out at the thought of being separated from him and yet everything that was human and passionate in her nature warned her that she was playing with fire.

*

The following morning Fiona learnt from Mrs. Meredith that the Duke and the Earl were leaving early for a long ride, which meant that she and Mary-Hose had The Castle to themselves for the day.

Looking out the window, Fiona saw that it was bright with sunshine and she decided that they must be out of doors as much as possible.

"Excuse me askin', miss," Mrs. Meredith said, breaking in on her thoughts, "but when you have the time, it would be real kind of you if you would call on old Granny."

"Who is she?" Fiona asked.

"That's what we always call her, miss, because she's the oldest woman in the Clan. She used to look after His Grace and Lord Ian when they were small and she loves to talk of the old days."

"Of course I will go and see her."

"She's nearly blind now, miss, and her mind wanders a bit, but I was told yesterday that she were askin' to see you. It'd be a real kindness if you would call on her."

"Of course I will," Fiona said. "Where does she live?

"Next to the East Gate, miss. It'll only take you about five minutes to walk there."

"Then I will call on her when Mary-Rose has her rest," Fiona promised.

"I'll send one of the men to tell her you'll be a-callin'," Mrs. Meredith said. "I know Granny'll be lookin' forward to it."

The sunshine, which had seemed so bright early in the morning, turned to rain and Mary-Rose could therefore not go for a walk as she usually did after her lessons.

Instead they played the piano, after which the child concentrated on making a drawing of Rollo, which she was doing as a surprise for the Duke.

"It's difficult to get his fur right, Aunt Fiona," she said after she had been drawing for a little while. "Let's go to the kennels so that I can look at Rollo and see what I am doing wrong."

"I expect Rollo will have gone with your uncle," Fiona replied. "Stay here. I will enquire."

She walked to the landing to look down to where there were two footmen on duty.

She called one, who ran up towards her, his kilt swinging as he did so and Fiona thought that no elaborate English livery could be as smart or as becoming.

"Has Rollo gone with His Grace?" she asked.

"Aye, miss," the footman replied. "I sees him runnin' behind the horses when his Lordship rode off."

"Thank you," Fiona said. "That is all I wanted to know."

She went back to Mary-Rose, who threw down her pencil, saying,

"I shall have to wait until tomorrow. I cannot do any more without seeing Rollo."

"Shall I read to you, dearest?" Fiona suggested. "Or shall we go and explore the library?"

Mary-Rose brightened.

"That would be fun! Uncle Aiden has lots and lots of books and some of them have pictures in them."

"Then let's go and see what we can find," Fiona proposed.

They found a book that contained drawings of dogs, which amused Mary-Rose. She talked about it all through luncheon and took it to bed with her when she went to lie down.

"I want you to try to sleep," Fiona urged, "so we will put the book beside you and it will be there when you wake up."

"I want to find if there is a picture in it where the dog looks as beautiful as Rollo."

"I am sure that would be impossible," Fiona smiled.

She tucked the little girl in comfortably, kissed her and pulled the curtains over the window.

"Don't be longer than an hour, Aunt Fiona," Mary-Rose begged.

"No, of course not," Fiona agreed. "I promise you I will come back exactly at half-past two."

"I will be very good," Mary-Rose promised.

As she closed the door, Fiona hurried to her own bedroom and picked up a light shawl to put round her shoulders.

It was no longer raining, but the sky was overcast and, instead of going bare-headed as she would have done on a sunny day, she pinned on a small straw hat that went with her gown of blue cotton trimmed with little frills of *broderie anglaise*.

It had taken Fiona many hours of work, but she knew that although the gown had cost her very little, it was exceedingly becoming and she hoped that the Duke would see her in it later when he returned from his ride.

Carrying an umbrella, she went down the wide marble staircase that led to the front door and walked away in the direction of the East Gate.

There was a good deal of ground for her to cover because this part of The Castle walls stretched out a long way to the East and she passed both the Falconer's Tower and the Abbott's Tower, which she and Mary-Rose had explored together.

She found the little lodge and the door was ajar.

"Come in," a quavering old voice called when she knocked and she found a very small white-haired old woman seated in a chair by the fireside.

"You must excuse me not getting' up, Miss," Granny said, "but I canna manage to stand on my own two legs by myself these days."

"Please don't move," Fiona said. "I will sit beside you."

She found a chair and sat down, noting as she did so that the room was spotlessly clean and was filled with little pieces of china, most of which contained bunches of faded white heather and small mementoes, which she was sure were part of the old woman's youth.

They talked for some time and then Fiona said,

"I am very sorry to learn of how His Grace lost his wife. It must be very sad for everyone to know that the mystery has never been solved."

"That's true enough," Granny said in her quavering voice. "But 'twas not a happy marriage. I knew that as soon as his Lordship, as he was then, brings home his bride."

"How did you know that?" Fiona enquired and realised as she spoke that it was a stupid question.

She was quite certain that Granny was what the Scots call 'fey'. There was something about her that Fiona instinctively recognised.

Perhaps it was the way she spoke or perhaps it was that the perceptiveness which was so much a part of her was there for anyone to see if they looked for it.

"Her Ladyship was not the right person to be the wife of the chief of the Clan," Granny persisted.

There was silence for a moment nand then Fiona asked,

"I feel that you can see things that other people cannot. Have you any idea where the Duchess can be?"

"Many have asked me that," Granny replied, "but the pain and anguish of her passin' blinds my eye."

"Pain and anguish?" Fiona questioned.

The old woman did not speak and she asked after a moment in a voice that trembled,

"Are you saying that – she met her death – violently?"

Again there was silence.

Then at last Granny said,

"Her spirit cries out for vengeance!"

Fiona drew in her breath.

She was afraid of her own thoughts and now she wished that she had not asked questions.

The old woman seemed to sink into her chair. Her eyes were closed, almost as if she had fallen asleep.

"I think I must go now," Fiona said.

She felt, when Granny opened her eyes, as if the old woman had come back to her from a very long way away, from another world that she could not enter.

"I was listenin', as I've listened afore, to her Ladyship cryin' for mercy," she said. "She received none and 'vengeance is mine, I will repay, saith the Lord'."

"Goodbye," Fiona said a little breathlessly. "Goodbye and I will come and see you again one day soon."

She moved towards the door, but the old woman did not speak or seem to notice that she was leaving.

Outside in the fresh air, Fiona felt as if she was coming out of a trance. She wanted to shake herself as if to be free of what she had just heard.

'The old woman's mind is wandering,' she said to herself, but she knew that she was upset and frightened by what she had just heard.

If Granny believed that the Duchess had been murdered, which indeed was what Fiona already half-suspected, it immediately evoked the question of who had murdered her – and why.

She began to walk very quickly back towards The Castle.

'I will not think about it,' she mused.

She tried to tell herself that the old woman had been influenced by the gossip she had heard, which must have been repeated by those who visited her.

"It's not true! It's not true!" Fiona cried in her heart.

But insidiously the question was there – who else but her husband had any reason for disposing of the Duchess? Who else found her impossible to live with?

Fighting her thoughts, Fiona hurried on, holding her shawl tightly about her as if in some way it protected her, although it was no longer cold.

She glanced up at the sky and saw that, although the wind had dropped, there was undoubtedly rain in the clouds above The Castle.

She felt as if the greyness of it was echoed in her heart and she recognised that old Granny's words had made everything seem dark and menacing.

'I am too sensible, too intelligent to listen to the meanderings of an old woman!' Fiona thought.

And yet she could hear the quavering old voice saying,

"Vengeance is mine, I will repay, saith the Lord."

She had almost reached The Castle when she saw someone walking towards her and realised that it was Lady Morag.

She was the last person Fiona wished to see at this moment and she had the idea that Lady Morag must have seen her from her house, moving across the ground towards the East Gate and was curious as to why she had gone in that direction.

'She behaves as if she owns the place!' Fiona told herself angrily.

She wondered if in fact it was Lady Morag who had put the idea of the Duchess being murdered into old Granny's mind.

'She is a mischief-maker, that is one thing for certain!' Fiona thought. 'I must be very careful what I say to her.'

Then she realised that Lady Morag was hurrying towards her in an unusual manner.

As she reached her, the older woman said breathlessly,

"I am so glad to have found you, Miss Windham! I have just called at The Castle to see if you were there. I understand that naughty little niece of yours, Mary-Rose, has been seen going into the Guard Tower!"

"The Guard Tower?" Fiona exclaimed in astonishment. "I am sure that is untrue. Mary-Rose has been told over and over again never to go near it."

"Nevertheless, I am afraid it's the truth," Lady Morag said, "and when I enquired, they said that Mary-Rose came out this way some minutes ago!"

"But the Guard Tower is dangerous!" Fiona cried.

"Very dangerous!" Lady Morag agreed. "I think we had better hurry and see what she is doing without wasting any more time."

"Yes, of course."

As she spoke, she began to run across the grass towards where the Guard Tower was situated on the Northern side of The Castle.

As she did so, she realised that Lady Morag was following her and she hoped frantically that Mary-Rose would not hurt herself in the Tower or get into a position from which she would have to be rescued.

She was well aware that Lady Morag would make the very worst of the situation and undoubtedly would use the fact that she had left Mary-Rose alone to accuse her of being an unsuitable person to look after the child.

Apart from this, the Duke had been so insistent that the Guard Tower was dangerous that Fiona was in reality very frightened.

It was not far to the Tower and, when Fiona reached it, she saw that the door that led into it was open.

This was not unusual for the hinges had rotted away and the door lay at a kind of drunken angle against the stonework.

"Mary-Rose must have gone up on the roof," Lady Morag said.

Fiona did not answer, but it struck her that this was indeed quite probable.

It was very unlike the child to be so naughty, but she had been thrilled by the story that her father had told her of how he and her uncle had defied their Tutor and climbed up onto the roof of the Guard Tower, where he could not fetch them down to do their lessons.

She had talked about it several times when they first arrived at The Castle, but recently there had been so many other things to distract her mind that Fiona thought that she must have forgotten the tale.

Without wasting time in talking, she started to climb up the stone stairs.

As in most Towers, they twisted round a centre structure with only arrow-slits on the outside walls to admit any light.

She climbed to the first floor of the tower and then saw very clearly why the Duke had said it was unsafe.

Through the open entrance of what must have been the first room, she could see that the floor had collapsed completely and was hanging down.

The beams that supported it and the wooden boards that had been affixed to them were held only by their attachment to the opposite wall.

A long way below them there appeared to be only darkness.

Without speaking, aware that Lady Morag was just behind her, Fiona started to climb again.

The stairs were worn with the footsteps of ages and Fiona, holding up her skirt with both hands, could not move very quickly.

Round and round the stairs twisted and now she thought that she must almost have reached the top.

It was then that she saw another door and through this she could see that the same decay had happened on this floor also.

The floor had not collapsed entirely as it had below, but it had become detached from the nearest wall and slanted at an angle, several of the boards obviously having slipped away.

Fiona paused a moment and, because by now she was really frightened, she called out,

"Mary-Rose! *Mary-Rose*!"

Her voice rang out, echoing round the stone walls and sounding strange and eerie.

There was no answer and she called again.

"Mary-Rose! Where are you? Answer me!"

"She will not answer you because she is not here!" Lady Morag said suddenly.

Fiona, who had tipped her head back as she had called, turned her face to find that Lady Morag was standing just behind her.

"What are you saying?" she asked. "You told me that she was here."

A smile curved Lady Morag's thin lips.

"I thought it was the easiest way to get you where I wanted you," she replied.

The manner in which she spoke made Fiona stare at her incredulously.

Then she said quickly,

"You don't know what you are saying and you have no right to bring me here under false pretences. As a joke it is in very poor taste."

"It is not a joke," Lady Morag replied. "I have brought you here to be rid of you!"

As she spoke, she reached out both her arms and Fiona gave a little cry.

She made as if to step aside, but she was too late.

"*Die*!" Lady Morag cried. "Die, as Janet died! And no one will ever find you!"

Her voice rose to a shriek as she spoke and even as it flashed through Fiona's mind that she was mad, she felt Lady Morag's hands pressing her forwards, pushing her with a strength against which she had no defence.

She felt herself falling. Then, with a last desperate effort to save herself, she stretched out her arms in an attempt to try to grasp the floor sloping down from the opposite wall of the tower.

It was only because she was fit and well and her will compelled her body to make the effort that she felt her fingers clutch the sloping floor near the bottom and then, as they slipped, she dug them into the narrow gap between two boards.

As she did so, her weight, slight though she was, made the broken floor creak and groan.

For a moment Fiona thought it would crash with her into the depths below, but surprisingly it held, although half her body was dangling in the air.

For a moment she could not think – dazed by the impact against the hard edge of the wood, she could only instinctively dig her fingers farther in between the boards and pray that she could hold on.

It was then that behind her she heard Lady Morag snarl,

"Fall! *Fall!* You have to die! You shall not live!"

For a moment Fiona felt that she might faint from the sheer horror of what was happening to her.

Her precarious hold on the floor and the venom in Lady Morag's voice did not seem real but part of a nightmare.

Then she thought of the Duke and knew that she had found the secret of his wife's death, but only if she remained alive could she tell him.

Because her love for him gave her strength, she screamed,

"Help! *Help!*"

She heard her voice ring out at first weakly and then, as she knew that she wanted help not only for herself but for the man she loved, she managed to make her cry louder.

"Help! Save me! Help!"

There was a strange silence from Lady Morag and Fiona wondered if she had run away.

She wanted to turn her head to look, but she did not dare.

Her hat had fallen off and her shoes were slipping from her feet but she had a feeling that the slightest unguarded movement might make the whole floor collapse as she had thought it must do when she had first flung herself against it.

There was what had been a window a little way above her, but the stones below it had crumbled away so that it was larger and longer than the arrow-slit that it had once been and let in a great deal more light.

Through it she could see the sky and she told herself that if anyone was listening it would carry her voice out into the open.

"Help! *Help!*" she cried again.

Then, as she did so, she realised why Lady Morag had been so quiet.

A large stone, obviously having broken away from the wall, hit the floor just above her hands and rolled over her fingers and down past her body.

For a second or so there was no sounds then far below a splash of water.

"That is where you will drown," Lady Morag cried. "Let yourself go, you fool! There will be no one to save you and I will stone you until you do fall!"

She must have gone in search of another stone, for her voice seemed to die away as she spoke and once again Fiona was shouting for help.

She cried out despairingly, knowing that if Lady Morag's aim with the next stone was more accurate it would be hard for her to keep her hold on the boards.

Already her arms were aching and her fingers had begun to feel numb.

'Someone must hear me!' she thought despairingly and then screamed with pain as another stone hit her in the middle of her back.

"*Die!*" Lady Morag screamed. "*Die, as Janet died!*"

*

The Duke, riding with the Earl through the entrance gate, saw the Major Domo staring up at a window of Lady Morag's house.

He glanced up perfunctorily and was on the point of riding on when he saw behind a closed window a small figure and recognised it as being Mary-Rose.

He turned his horse and rode towards the Major Domo.

"What is happening, Malcolm?" he asked.

"I don't rightly know, Your Grace," the man answered, "but apparently Miss Mary-Rose is locked up in her Ladyship's house."

"Is there no one there?" the Duke enquired.

"I understand her Ladyship's servants, like most of ours, have gone off to the rehearsals for the games, Your Grace."

"Oh yes, of course," the Duke said. "I saw them there. But where is Lady Morag?"

"I understand, Your Grace, from the lodge-keeper, although I think he must have been mistaken, that he saw her and Miss Windham climbing up the steps of the Guard Tower a few minutes ago."

"The Guard Tower?" the Duke exclaimed incredulously. "But they know how dangerous it is!"

"There is something wrong here," interposed the Earl, who had been listening. "Let's go and investigate."

He started to ride across the grass as he spoke and the Duke followed him, only saying over his shoulder,

"Get Miss Mary-Rose out, Malcolm, even if you have to break the door down!"

The two riders reached the Guard Tower and, without wasting time in conversation, the Duke threw himself off his horse and ran up the steps to the open door.

As he did so, he heard Fiona's scream and Lady Morag's voice, so distorted that it was hard to recognise, shouting,

"Die! Die, as Janet died!"

The Duke, followed by the Earl, began to climb the stairs.

As they reached the opening on the first floor, the Duke stopped and looked up to see Fiona's gown trailing over the edge of the sloping floor above.

He could also, by twisting his head upwards, see Lady Morag, a large stone in her raised hand, standing in the opening of the floor above.

"*Stop!*" he cried. "Stop that immediately!"

"She has to die!" Lady Morag shrieked. "She is trying to take you away from me. She has to die!"

"What in God's name is happening?" the Earl asked the Duke.

"Go up and stop Morag," the Duke ordered. "I must reach Fiona from the other side of the Tower."

He pushed past the Earl and started to descend the steps as quickly as he had climbed them.

The Earl, without wasting time asking questions, started to climb upwards to find that Rollo, who had followed them up the stairs, was now going up ahead of him. The dog had not realised that his master had begun to descend the stairs.

Only as the Earl almost reached the top did he hear a snarl and see that Rollo, with his hackles raised, was growling at Lady Morag.

She was shrinking away from him, her eyes wild and distended, staring at the dog with horror.

"*Go away!*" she ordered. "Go away!"

Then, lifting the stone she held in her hand, she flung it at the dog's head.

With a ferocious bark that seemed to fill the air, Rollo sprang.

The next second, before the Earl could move or do
anything to prevent it, Lady Morag, screaming shrilly,
toppled over the edge to fall into the darkness of the
water below.

Chapter Seven

A servant came into the room to hand the Countess of Selway a note on a silver salver.

"From Rannock Castle, my Lady," he said, "and the groom is waiting in case there is an answer."

At the other end of the breakfast table Fiona felt herself grow tense as she watched the Countess take the note from the salver and open it.

This she did with a grace that was characteristic and, watching her downcast eyes, Fiona thought as she had often thought before how attractive the Earl's mother was.

She had been beautiful when she was young and now her face had a sweetness that expressed her nature. In many ways she reminded Fiona of her own mother.

The Countess, however, was little more than fifty and Fiona often forgot her age and talked to her as if she was a contemporary.

After what seemed a very long time, the Countess raised her eyes and said to the servant,

"There will be no answer."

As he withdrew she looked at Fiona with a hint of mischief in her expression and said,

"I know that you are consumed with curiosity."

"Do you expect me to – feel anything – else?" Fiona asked.

The Countess turned to Mary-Rose, who had just finished her breakfast.

"Will you do something for me, dearest child," she asked, "and feed my birds?"

Mary-Rose gave a little cry of excitement.

"Can I do that all by myself?"

"I feel that you will manage it just as well as I would, but don't forget the water."

"I'll remember everything!" Mary-Rose said excited-ly, getting down from the table.

She would have run from the room, but she stopped by the Countess's chair to say,

"It's so lovely being here with you."

Then she was gone and they could hear her small feet pattering down the passage.

The Countess laughed.

"I have a feeling that Mary-Rose will be spending a great deal of time with me in the future and I cannot tell you how much I am looking forward to it."

Fiona did not reply and after a moment the Countess added,

"This is a very long letter from Torquil, so I will tell you briefly what it contains."

She looked down at the letter for a moment and then went on,

"First, Lady Morag's body has been taken North, so that it can be buried at her home with the rest of her MacDonald relations."

Fiona drew in her breath but she did not speak, and the Countess continued,

"The Duchess's funeral will take place tomorrow with great pomp and ceremony. Torquil says that as far as he can ascertain, everyone of any importance in Scotland will be present."

"I thought that would happen," Fiona said almost beneath her breath.

"It will be, of course," the Countess carried on, "their way of making an apology and I only hope that the conscience of most of those present prickles them when they remember their behaviour of the last few years."

"I am sure that the Duke deeply appreciates your son's loyalty and yours," Fiona murmured. "It is all he has had for so long."

"I have loved Aiden ever since he was a small boy," the Countess said, "and I knew that he could never have committed a crime so uncivilised as murder. Although I can assure you that by the way Janet behaved, she often deserved a good beating."

The Countess spoke with a note of anger in her voice and then said quickly,

"But we must not speak ill of the dead. Now everything that happened in the past can be forgotten and Aiden can start a new life – "

She paused for a moment and then added,

" – with you!"

Fiona felt the colour rushing into her face and instinctively she looked over her shoulder as if to make sure that there was nobody else in the room.

"It's all right," the Countess said, "but we must be very discreet and the person who is most insistent on that is Aiden himself. That is why we three, you, I and Mary-Rose are leaving for London tomorrow morning."

"*For London?*" Fiona exclaimed in astonishment.

"Aiden will join us as soon as it is possible for him to do so," the Countess said. "The one thing about which he is determined is that you should not be talked about."

"But if we – stayed at Rannock House – " Fiona faltered.

"But we will not be staying at Rannock House," the Countess interrupted. "The mansion that has been in the Selway family for years may not be as impressive or contain such fabulous treasures, but I assure you it is very comfortable."

"You are very – kind."

"I feel as if Aiden is my son and I so want him to be happy. And that is what I know he is going to be."

Fiona blushed again, but before she could say anything the Countess went on,

"We shall be very busy in London, you and I. You will not have much time to buy your trousseau."

For a moment Fiona's eyes widened with excitement.

Then she said hesitatingly,

"I am – afraid that I cannot – afford a very extensive trousseau at the – moment."

"It will be my wedding present and Torquil's to Aiden," the Countess said with a smile. "I have often wondered, if he ever married again, what I could give him that he could possibly want and now I know the answer."

"B-but – please," Fiona protested, "you must not – do that."

"It is something I have every intention of doing, Fiona, so don't let's argue about it. I know in the new life that you and Aiden are going to spend together you will want to look your very best."

Again there was a mischievous look in her brown eyes as she added,

"Remember, he is a very handsome man."

To Fiona it seemed impossible that the terrible scene she had enacted with Lady Morag had actually taken place and yet, when she could think about it coherently, she knew that, terrifying though it had been, it had proved a blessing in disguise.

When the Duke had pulled her to safety and held her close in his arms, as they sat on the broken stones of what had once been a window of the Tower, she had thought that he had drawn her up from a horrible and terrifying Hell into a Heaven where nothing existed except themselves.

She had clung so desperately to her precarious hold on the boards of the sloping floor that even when she realised that she was safe it was hard to believe that she was not still battling to save not only herself but also the Duke.

'I must not fall! *I must not!*' she had told herself over and over again in her mind as she waited, with her whole body tense, for the next stone that Lady Morag would hurl at her.

She was afraid that if it struck her on the head it might render her unconscious. Then she would fall as the mad woman intended and would disappear as the Duchess had disappeared in the dark waters beneath her.

It was only later that Fiona was to learn that while the moat had been dragged after the Duchess had vanished, no one had thought of the water that seeped into the foundations of the Guard Tower.

It had in fact been only a few feet deep, but, when Lady Morag had pushed her sister into it, the Duchess had hit her head against the stony bottom and had been knocked unconscious.

She had therefore died from drowning, as was ascertained when they finally found what remained of her body.

When she was first rescued, all Fiona could think of was that she was close to the Duke and that she loved him until there seemed to be nothing else in the world but him and the security of his arms.

"You are safe, my precious," he said, "but I might have lost you!"

There was so much pain in his voice that Fiona wished to comfort him and yet it was impossible for her to speak.

The shock of what she had been through had taken her voice away and afterwards she thought that she had been only half-conscious, yet at the same time vividly aware of the closeness of the Duke and her love for him.

It took some time before the Earl could fetch men with ladders and ropes to rescue them, but Fiona felt that if they stayed where they were for an eternity, it would not be too long.

The Duke had carried her back to her room and laid her down on the bed. Only when she had realised that he was about to leave her did she manage to whisper tremulously in a voice that did not seem to be her own,

"Y-you – are – safe!"

She could think only of his danger and not of what had been her own.

"I am safe now and in the future, thanks to you," the Duke said in his deep voice.

Mrs. Meredith was in the room, so he could not say any more, but he lifted up to his lips Fiona's cold hand with its bruised fingers and broken nails.

Then he left her.

The physician was sent for, but he merely told Fiona to rest and try to sleep.

He gave her some medicine, but she told Mrs. Meredith how to prepare some of her own herbs, after which she slept peacefully and dreamlessly.

The following day she wanted to get up, but Mrs. Meredith said that on the Duke's instructions she was to stay in bed.

"You don't want to be round, miss, and that's a fact!" she said. "They're raisin' her Ladyship's body and Her Grace's from the foot of the Guard Tower and His Grace's instructions are that everybody should keep away."

Fiona shuddered.

There was something horrible in thinking of the two sisters lying together dead in the water and of the terrible trouble that had been causcd by the Duchess's disappearance.

Now she knew that the Duke was free of the suspicions that had encompassed him like a dark cloud for so long and which had grown more menacing year by year.

"Now those who ostracised him will learn how wrong they were,' Fiona thought and she was smiling as she fell asleep.

Fiona was not surprised on the following day when Mrs. Meredith informed her that arrangements had been made for her and Mary-Rose to stay with the Earl's mother and for them to leave immediately.

She had hoped that she would be able to see the Duke alone, but when she left her bedroom wearing her travelling clothes, to walk with Mary-Rose into the drawing room, she realised why it would be impossible.

The Duke was there, but there were six other men with him, all the Chieftains of the nearest Clans and those who had deliberately denied him their friendship since the Duchess's disappearance.

The Duke introduced them to Mary-Rose and then to her.

"I am sending my niece to stay with Selway's mother until all this unpleasantness is over," he explained.

"I think that is very wise of you, Strathrannock," an elderly man said. "The Castle is not a place for women at the moment."

He looked at Fiona as he spoke and she thought she saw a glint of admiration in his elderly eyes. There was no doubt, moreover, that the other gentlemen were looking at her with curiosity.

"Goodbye, Miss Windham," the Duke said in a carefully controlled voice. "Thank you very much for bringing Mary-Rose here from the South. I am only sorry that you should leave with such unpleasant memories."

"All the same my visit has been extremely interesting, Your Grace," Fiona said quietly.

She knew this little scene was being enacted so that the Duke's neighbours would not question her presence in The Castle or attach any particular significance to it.

"Goodbye, Uncle Aiden," Mary-Rose said as the Duke picked her up in his arms. "I want to come back soon and go on with my fishing. Donald says I shall soon be as good as you, if not better!"

There was general laughter at this and they left the drawing room with the Earl, amongst a general expression of goodwill and good wishes for their journey.

Downstairs there were two carriages waiting, one to convey Fiona and Mary-Rose, the other loaded with luggage and also containing one of Mrs. Meredith's most trusted maids to attend to their needs.

"Enjoy yourselves with my mother," the Earl said as a footman put a rug over their knees, "and will you give her this note from me? Tell her I will keep in touch and let her know of everything that happens."

Fiona knew the message was meant for her too.

Then, when she took from the Earl's hand, the note he had spoken about, she found that there was not one envelope but two.

She waited until they had driven away with Mary-Rose and could no longer see The Castle before she looked down at what she held in her hands, to know with a leap of her heart that one note was for her.

She opened it and found that it contained just three words – three words that told her everything she wanted to know.

"I love you!"

After that she knew that she would have to rely on news of the Duke from the letters that Torquil wrote so dutifully to his mother.

She realised that it was a sensible arrangement, but at the same time every nerve in her body vibrated at the thought of him and ached with her need to be close to him and to hear his voice.

She was, however, sensible enough to know that for the next few days at the Earl's home she must rest and get over the shock of what had happened.

Her sister, Rosemary, who had been very experienced in treating people for all sorts of ailments, had always said that it was more important to treat shock than to bandage injuries.

"The body will usually heal itself," she had said in her soft voice, "but the mind is something that needs special care and is of greater consequence than anything else."

Because Fiona wanted to be well for the Duke and also to look her best for him, she allowed the Countess to persuade her to rise late in the mornings and to rest, as Mary-Rose did, after luncheon.

The Earl's castle was very different from the Duke's.

Being comparatively modern, it was light and airy with a very pleasant view over a valley and the garden was filled with flowers, which were the Countess's special hobby, apart from her aviary of birds.

"Flowers are beautiful," she said to Fiona, "and we all need beauty in our lives, especially when we have come in contact, as you have, with the ugliness of human nature."

Looking back, Fiona now realised that she had always thought there was something unpleasant or, as one might say, 'ugly', about Lady Morag.

She had instinctively distrusted her from the first moment they had met.

Yet in a way she could understand her excessive twisted love for the Duke, which had driven her to the point where she could deliberately destroy her own sister because she wanted him.

Fiona had pieced together like a jigsaw puzzle the process by which Lady Morag had, once she had come to live at The Castle after she was widowed, deliberately stirred up trouble between the Duke and her sister.

It had not been difficult, because, the Countess had told Fiona, Janet MacDonald had been very neurotic and hysterical.

"No one in their senses would have married her to a man as sensitive and intelligent as Aiden," she had said, "but the old Duke was obsessed by his family history and the history of Scotland. Janet's father offered him as a Marriage Settlement the return of land that the MacDonalds had stolen from the Rannocks way back in the dim ages."

The Countess had given a little expression of disgust as she added,

"I often think that those who care so much about history forget how deeply ordinary people suffer in the course of it."

Fiona learnt that the Earl had told his mother that he had wished to marry her himself, but realised that his suit was impossible.

"You are just the sort of girl I would like Torquil to marry," the Countess admitted frankly one evening when they were alone after Mary-Rose had gone to bed, "but I think in some ways it will do him good to wait a little longer before he finds the right person."

"I do hope he does," Fiona murmured, although she was surprised at the Countess's philosophical attitude towards her son.

"Torquil," his mother explained, "is in some ways very young where women are concerned. The Duke, because he has suffered, is more mature, although they are almost the same age in years."

"Do you think that such suffering is important?' Fiona asked.

"I think that Aiden will make a far better husband than he would have made in the past," the Countess answered. "I am sure, now that he can choose a woman he loves for his wife, that he will make her very happy."

"He is so – wonderful!" Fiona sighed, "and if he was of no consequence whatsoever – just an ordinary man – I should feel– exactly the same about him."

The Countess smiled.

"That is what I hoped you would say," she said, "and what in fact I know you feel. I have always wanted Aiden to be loved for himself and he really is a very special person."

That was the truth, Fiona told herself, and she hated, although it seemed foolish, the knowledge that the Duke's private train was taking them farther and farther from him every mile that it steamed South.

Mary-Rose, however, was delighted to be back on the train.

She remembered the Stewards and the others in attendance whom she had met before, and insisted on shaking hands with the engine driver and his assistant.

"Am I not lucky," she asked the Countess, "to have an uncle who has his own train and the biggest castle in the whole of Scotland?"

"Very lucky," the Countess agreed.

"I'll tell you a secret, but you'll not tell anybody?" Mary-Rose went on.

"I promise," the Countess answered.

"I think your castle is really nicer than Uncle Aiden's, but we must not tell him so, must we?"

"No, of course not," the Countess nodded. "That would be unkind."

However, when she was alone with Fiona she said,

"I am going to suggest to Aiden when we see him that Mary-Rose comes to live with me as soon as you are married. I would love to have her and as our castle is so near, you will be in constant touch with each other."

"Please – please," Fiona begged, "you are going too – hastily. The Duke has not asked me to marry him yet – so I cannot plan – ahead as if it was – inevitable. Suppose he – changes his mind?"

"I think that is unlikely" the Countess said with a smile, "but we will wait and see. If, however, you think you can wait for your trousseau, you are very much mistaken! Clothes take time and we must be ready to do exactly what Aiden wants."

It was an excitement she had certainly not expected, to choose what she was sure were the most beautiful gowns anyone had ever dreamt of, while the Countess insisted on spending what Fiona thought was an astronomical amount on a trousseau that, as she said, "might have been made for a Princess".

"A Duchess is just as important," the Countess reminded her, "and, as you are English, you are well aware that the Scots will be very critical."

"You are making me nervous," Fiona protested. "Suppose I fail the Duke? Suppose I do all the wrong things and the Scots – disapprove of me?"

The Countess laughed.

"I am quite sure that your husband will look after you, my dear, and prevent you from making any mistakes. As to criticisms, as long as he thinks you are exactly what he wants in a wife, why should you worry what anyone else thinks?"

'She is quite right,' Fiona thought.

At the same time, as the days passed and there was no sign of the Duke arriving in London, she began to feel a little tremor of fear within her that perhaps he had changed his mind.

They had a letter from the Earl, saying that the funeral had been very impressive and it had been impossible for all the important mourners to get into the small Kirk.

But they had all gathered in The Castle and had made such a fuss of the Duke that it had been difficult for him not to laugh at their hypocrisy and tell them exactly what he thought of them.

The Earl had written,

"Aiden accepted the situation with great dignity and never once showed that he had been hurt or angered by their unjust suspicions which had haunted him in the past. I think a large number of our neighbours will doubtless be more generous-minded in the future."

"I hope so too," Fiona said when the Countess had finished reading the letter. "There is no doubt that they behaved abominably and only somebody who is very big in every way would ignore it."

"Aiden is behaving exactly as I expected him to do," the Countess said. "Everything that concerned the Duchess is best forgotten. Remember that or you will find yourself starting new feuds and there are quite enough in Scotland as it is without anyone adding to them."

"You are right," Fiona agreed. "I will try to forget, but I hate injustice."

"We all do!" the Countess remarked. "But like Aiden you have to be big and accept things as they are, not as you would wish them to be."

Fiona hoped that she could live up to such ideals. At the same time all she wanted was to see the Duke and be sure that he really loved her as she loved him.

'Perhaps,' she told herself in the darkness of the night, 'now that he is free, he will think it more amusing to go back to the Social world from which he had been excluded since his wife's disappearance.'

She knew that he would be welcomed with open arms, for there were not many rich, handsome and eligible young Dukes and all the ambitious mothers would be hoping that he would fancy their daughters.

'I am nobody of any consequence,' Fiona thought unhappily.

Yet the love she had for the Duke and he for her had been so overwhelming and irresistible that they had both been swept off their feet. Could any other considerations be of importance when all that mattered was that they should be together again?

Because she was human she was not quite sure and the Countess complained that she was getting thinner and that her new gowns would have to be taken in at the waist, which would be a terrible nuisance since so many of them were already finished.

'Please, God, make him go on loving me,' Fiona prayed every night.

*

She was sitting in the drawing room of the house in London late one afternoon and was working on a piece of embroidery that she intended as a present for her hostess.

The Countess had taken Mary-Rose to the zoo and Fiona was thinking that they were later than she had expected when she heard the door open.

"Oh, here you are!" she exclaimed, finishing the stitch she was making in her embroidery. "I am glad you are back!"

"That is what I wanted to hear you say," a deep voice replied, and Fiona gave a startled little cry and rose to her feet.

It was the Duke who stood just inside the room and for a moment she felt that he looked like a stranger.

Then she realised that he not only looked younger and happier than he had ever done before but also she had never seen him except dressed as a Scot.

Now, in the conventional dress of an English gentleman, he looked exceedingly smart and elegant and yet somehow different.

They stood gazing at each other and it seemed to Fiona as if the Duke's eyes were searching her face, looking deep below the surface as if he sought for her very soul.

Then quite simply, without saying any more, he just held out his arms.

She made a little sound that was all her lips could utter and ran towards him, wanting only to be close to him, to know that he was real and that he was really there.

His arms went round her and he pulled her almost roughly against him.

For a long moment he looked down at her face as if he could hardly believe what he saw, before his lips were on hers.

It was then that Fiona knew that all her apprehensions and her worries as to whether he really loved her had been unnecessary.

She knew by the touch of his lips how much he wanted her and how hard it had been for him to stay away from her so long.

The wonder and rapture she had known before when he kissed her seemed to sweep away everything but an ecstasy that made her feel as if they were no longer in the world but were carried away into a special Heaven that had always been there when he touched her.

She felt her whole body respond to him so that her heart was beating in time with his heart and her mind was part of his.

'I love you!' she wanted to shout, but it was quite unnecessary.

Only a love so strong, so omnipotent, so majestic and so divine could have united them so completely and so irrevocably.

At last, after time had stood still, the Duke raised his head.

"My precious, my darling!" he exclaimed, his voice deep and unsteady. "Do you still love me?"

"I intended to – ask you the same – question," Fiona whispered.

"You know the answer," the Duke replied, "but if you thought I was tardy in coming to you, please believe me that it was really impossible for me to get away until now."

"I – tried to – understand, but – I wanted you."

"Just as I wanted you!"

Now he was kissing her again and she saw a fire in his eyes and knew that he needed her with an intensity that was inexpressible.

The Duke kissed her until the breath was coming fitfully from between her lips and her eyes were shining like stars.

Then he said,

"Let me look at you. I would not have believed it possible, but you are even more beautiful than when I last saw you!"

"I – want to be – beautiful for – you," Fiona said, "and if I had known you were coming I would have taken more – trouble about my appearance."

"You look lovely as you are! So lovely that I am half-afraid you are part of a dream that will vanish and I will find that you never existed at all."

"I am not a – dream but very – real."

As Fiona spoke, she lifted her lips to his again, but, although he pulled her closer to him, he did not kiss her.

"We have so much to discover about each other," he said, "and now there is no reason to wait. We are being married tomorrow morning!"

"*Tomorrow* – morning?"

"Then I am taking you away."

"Where?"

"First to Paris, then to Rome."

Fiona made a little sound of excitement and the Duke asked,

"You will like that for your honeymoon?"

"It sounds – wonderful! At the same time, I will be happy – anywhere as – long as I am with – you."

"As I will be, but we are going abroad until the autumn and our marriage will only be announced just before we return."

He put his cheek against hers as he added,

"When we go back to Scotland, my darling, my country will give you the right sort of welcome. You will find it very different from what it has been up till now."

"Nothing is important in Scotland or anywhere else," Fiona said, "as long as you – love me and we are – together."

"You are quite certain of that?" the Duke asked. "I love you so much that I find it hard to express my feelings."

As he spoke, Fiona knew that he was telling her that for years he had bottled up everything he had thought and felt and had inflicted upon himself a reserve that would be hard to discard.

Then she knew that her love for him and his for her would be like sunshine dispersing the darkness of his dungeon.

As he had told her before, she had brought him light and now she had opened the door of his prison and he was free.

Words to express what he felt were unnecessary. What mattered was that they responded to each other and in their thoughts they were so close that each knew what the other was thinking.

"I love you!" Fiona murmured. "And when I am your wife I will be able to – tell you how – much."

She saw by the expression in the Duke's eyes that that was what he wanted her to say.

Then he was kissing her again, kissing her until her heart was beating as frantically as his and their need for each other burned like a fire within them both.

*

"It is so beautiful!" Fiona murmured.

"And so are you, my precious," the Duke replied.

Fiona smiled at him from the window where she had been looking at the dawn turning the City to gold.

They were staying on the outskirts of Rome in a palazzo which had been lent to them by one of the Duke's friends and below Fiona could see the Tiber, the roofs of the Eternal City and the great dome of St. Peter's.

In the pale morning sunshine the whole vista seemed to sparkle as if it was touched with a celestial light and the cypress trees in the garden were like human prayers pointing towards the cloudless blue of the sky.

From a huge painted and carved bed the Duke watched his wife, knowing that she was not aware that her body in its thin nightgown was silhouetted against the light.

He thought that none of the statues of the Goddesses which graced the grounds of the palazzo had a perfection to equal Fiona's and he felt a sudden throbbing in his temples which told him that her beauty stirred him as he had never been stirred before by any woman.

He thought to himself that he worshipped her for her beauty. At the same time what he loved about her was the depth and intensity of her love, which made her surrender herself to him completely and absolutely without reservation.

She was his as he had never expected or thought a woman could be.

Yet even in her surrender she still retained her individuality, so that she stimulated his mind and they were attuned in a way that he had not thought it possible to be.

"Oh, Aiden, you must come and look at the sun shining on the fountains," Fiona urged him. "It makes the whole place look unreal, as if we had stepped into a Fairyland."

She smiled as she spoke and added,

"And that is exactly what we have done. Come and look!"

"I have something else to do."

She turned her head in surprise.

"What is that?"

"I will tell you if you come here."

"I want you to see the fountains."

"And I want to see you."

She looked at him irresolutely, tempted to do what he wanted and yet wishing to have her own way.

"Come here!" the Duke said in his deep voice and now it was a command.

Because she could not disobey and had no wish to do so, Fiona ran back to the bed and, as she reached it, two strong arms pulled her into it and the Duke held her close again him.

"I cannot bear to let you leave me," he said, "not even for a moment."

"Oh, darling, when you say things like that, you make me so happy that I want to cry."

"If you cry on our honeymoon, I shall be very angry!" the Duke replied. "Besides, I dislike women who weep to get their own way."

"I will never do that," Fiona promised, "because your way is mine. It is a vow I made when we were married and one I intend to keep."

The Duke kissed her forehead.

"What is it about you," he asked, "that makes you so irresistible? I find it hard to think of anything else."

"Are you telling me you have forgotten Scotland?" Fiona teased.

"Almost," he admitted. "I have put it at the back of my mind and all I can think of is how soft and adorable you are, how much I want to kiss you and how impossible it is not to make love to you twenty-four hours a day."

There was a sincerity in the Duke's voice that was unmistakable and Fiona put her arm round his neck to whisper,

"I love you until at times I am frightened that I shall bore you by saying so over and over again. At the same time, my beloved wonderful husband, I think soon we must plan to go home."

"Why?" the Duke questioned.

"Because, although nothing could be more perfect than being here alone with you, I know there are things which you have to do which no one else can do for you. I also know that now that you are reinstated in the hearts of your countrymen, you must take your rightful place amongst them."

The Duke knew that she was talking sense.

Equally it astounded him that anyone so young and in a way so inexperienced in life should not only know what was right but actually suggest it before he did so himself.

"How do you know such things?" he asked aloud. "How are you so knowledgeable about the things that really matter?"

"If I am right, it is only where you are concerned," Fiona replied. "Because I love you, I want everything in your life to be perfect and that is what I shall try to make it"

With a little passionate gesture she pressed her lips against his shoulder before she went on,

"You have made me so happy. You have given me the sun, the moon and the stars to play with and you have made me aware that I am the luckiest woman in the world, but now we have to think about you."

"Scotland seems very far away," the Duke sighed against her hair.

"That is the greatest compliment you could ever pay me," Fiona replied. "At the same time, my dearest one, you are wanted there and I think you will find, because you have been out of things for so long, that there will be a thousand new duties piled upon you. Also – "

She paused.

"Also – ?" the Duke questioned.

"There is – another reason – for going – home!"

Her voice was so soft that he could barely hear what she said.

His arms tightened but he asked in an ordinary tone,

"Now what can that be?"

There was no answer and after a moment he asked very tenderly,

"Shall I guess?"

"Oh, Aiden, you *know* – and, darling, I want you to be glad."

"Glad! I am ecstatic, but, my precious, are you sure?"

"I think so – and it would be so wonderful if I could give you a son and a future Chieftain."

The Duke moved Fiona backwards so that her head was on the pillow and he was looking down at her.

"I suppose all men," he said slowly, "long to find the perfect, ideal woman whom they see in their dreams and all men, if they are honest, think cynically that it is impossible. But I have achieved the impossible – I possess perfection."

"That is what I – want you to – think," Fiona answered. "But please – do not probe too – deeply or you may find all the – flaws. Then you will be – disappointed."

"That will never happen."

Then he was kissing her with slow, burning kisses that awoke a fire in her to complement the one raging within himself.

It made Fiona feel, as she had felt before, that they were part of the beauty that surrounded them, part too of the beauty of love that lay within their hearts and seemed to grow deeper and deeper every day.

It was a love that she knew was unique and yet they had found it because each was the other half of the other and they were only complete when they were together.

The Duke's lips became more insistent, his hand was touching her body and she felt herself quiver with the ecstasy that was half-pleasure and half-pain that he always evoked within her.

She knew that he felt the same and the rapture they aroused in each other carried them into the cloudless sky that she had just seen from the window.

This was love.

This was living so that human beings became as Gods.

"*I love you!*" Fiona cried within her heart.

She knew that the Duke was saying the same to her without words and there was no need of them.

They had passed through deep waters to find each other.

It was love that had shown the way, a love over-whelming and irresistible that would help and sustain them through the years that lay ahead, so that they would never lose each other again.

OTHER BOOKS IN THIS SERIES

The Barbara Cartland Eternal Collection is the unique opportunity to collect all five hundred of the timeless beautiful romantic novels written by the world's most celebrated and enduring romantic author.

Named the Eternal Collection because Barbara's inspiring stories of pure love, just the same as love itself, the books will be published on the internet at the rate of four titles per month until all five hundred are available.

The Eternal Collection, classic pure romance available worldwide for all time.

Made in the USA
Monee, IL
13 January 2023

25197748R00132